Michael Butler

Driveshaft

WriteSideLeft
2019

ISBN: Print: 978-1-9161011-6-6
ISBN: eBook: 978-1-9161011-7-3
ISBN: Audiobook: 978-1-9161011-8

Compilation & Cover Design by S A Harrison
Photo by J Baker

Published by WriteSideLeft UK

www.writesideleft.com

Contents

Prologue 5

Driveshaft –Original Release 9

Annie's Café 73

Frank 77

Weirdo Academics 93

Finding Katherine 96

Lena in the Frame 115

What Day Is It? 121

Four, Possessed 125

The Shit Brown Volvo 131

The Road to Dungeness 135

The Cheapest Film Shoot in History 146

Ritzy Cinema or Classic? 158

Driveshaft Redux: A New Ending 164

Back to the Future Now 171

Epilogue 174

Prologue

Squashed. I was in that room in *Star Wars* where the walls and floor and ceiling close in on the heroes. They are about to be squashed but something saves them—can't remember what. Anyway, they get out. So did I. I got out. Escaped. A year unpaid sabbatical. I had to sign a document saying I'd go back. I knew I wouldn't go back but I signed it anyway. Tried to smile at the head-teacher as I signed the 'promise I'll return' forms. But I couldn't smile. It came out as a hybrid sneer/smile; a 'snile' or a 'smeer'. Anyway, I took the sabbatical.

Squashed. Teaching, you see, is a many-headed monster which can squash you mercilessly. Squashed you could well be, and there were plenty up for the job. Some squashed you by accident, some squashed you for kicks, some squashed you because that was just what they did, what they were programmed to do. The squashers were ubiquitous, legion; if you didn't keep an eye on yourself, you'd morph into one and start squashing. So, I took the sabbatical.

When you have a lot of it on your hands, time can be a great friend and a great enemy. You keep an eye on it, or rather, it keeps an eye on you. You become, one becomes, I became very precious, very protective of my time. Wasting it felt like a sin. I'm not religious but that is what it felt like. So, I was determined to use it wisely—time not sin—and try, try and try to forget about school.

Meanwhile, and it's a big meanwhile, an important meanwhile that is at the heart of things. Meanwhile, I had this thing for Margot Kidder. Who? It started—this thing—as a fascination when I was a teen. I first saw Margot in this slightly dodgy horror film called *The Amityville Horror*. The film is a bit of a stinker but worth watching just to see Margot doing some barre work while wearing little other than a shasta daisy behind her ear—right ear, and one white woollen leg-warmer—left leg. It's thirty-two minutes in—if you want to skip to the scene. It's memorable.

But as adolescence was swallowed up by adulthood, I sort of forgot about important stuff, like Margot, horror movies and leg warmers. Then me and Margot met up again when I read a book about the independent movie scene in 70s Hollywood. In *Easy Riders, Raging Bulls*, Margot gets decent coverage. She had a lot to say about the film industry and said it with some style. So, my interest was rekindled, my admiration broadened to appreciate Margot's mind—past and current—as well as her physical attributes—past. I started to watch and re-watch her movies, chiefly from the 70s and 80s, and interviews from various eras. So, the fascination grew again; this time I fell for a composite of Margots, made up of the words and images that had captivated me for months—'Margot Kidder', if you like.

Back to time then. Like I say, there was a lot of it on my hands so, I tried to use it wisely. Some folk study philosophy, some politics, some are worried about green issues or the rise of the right; I studied, worried about and became an expert on Margot Kidder. I became a devotee. I dived into Margot's world, felt a strong, no overwhelming, compulsion to write about her. So, I wrote. But I could never finish anything. At first, I attempted a sort of biography. Didn't finish it. Then I introduced some fictional strands which rendered the biography uneven and abstract. Didn't finish that. Then, I went all out for fiction. I tried to write a kind of play/novel of Margot's life in the early 70s in California. I based her character on what I'd read, researched, watched and imagined. It was okay, but I got stuck. So, I listened to a writer who said that if you were stuck 'throw in a dead body'. So, I did. I introduced a gangster subplot that, although fun to play with, just got in the way. So, I didn't finish that either.

I'd almost given up on finishing anything that I started about Margot. There are a couple of hundred thousand words sitting on my hard-drive, gathering dust and crying out—or maybe just protesting mildly—to be knocked into shape. Anyway, I shelved the writing, and started to do mundane things like run and swim and go to the gym. I even planned a holiday. What kind of a sabbatical was this turning into? I wondered. I still tried to write something 'Margotcentric', occasionally rejigging paragraphs, looking for new articles on the net, stuff like that, but I was always going backwards or sideways, never forward.

Then I discovered something or, perhaps more accurately, something discovered me.

One Friday night I was trawling for Margot related stuff on the net when something odd popped up. On YouTube I stumbled upon a film called *Driveshaft* starring Margot Kidder. It had never been there, or anywhere, online before and was nowhere on Margot's CV. I watched it, alone at first, and was staggered. After this first viewing I wanted to find out as much about *Driveshaft* as I possibly could. But nothing. There was not a trace of information anywhere. Yes, I looked there too; you wouldn't be able to name a place that I didn't look. Not one digital stone was left unturned. The appearance of the film was an oddity which led to a mystery which morphed into, well, something else.

What follows is about *Driveshaft*, I tried my best to reproduce the film in the form of a script as it has now disappeared completely. More importantly, however, it is about what happened after I watched the film—the aftermath. The aftermath ended up being stranger than the film itself. It all took place over a few wet and dark days in November, not so long ago; wet, dark, cold and otherworldly.

I dedicate what follows to my great friends, Frank, Katherine and, of course, Lena. Frank for his strength, kindness and wisdom, Katherine for same and for helping me to record the *Driveshaft* script in such detail and Lena for being, well, Lena. Ultimately, though, this is for Margot Kidder. I was able, at long last, to finish something about you, Margot.

Driveshaft–Original Release

Lena slid on top of me. I tensed up and then relaxed. She felt reassuringly heavy and warm and good. After nuzzling the back of my neck for a time, she looked up at the laptop at the end of the bed and groaned. Then she did a half-decent scratchy, North American accent.

'Oh, Benny, you found me again, baby. I've been so lonesome without ya. It's been—what?—ten minutes since you thought about me? Oh, come to me, come to Margot's bosom, my little Superman.'

Lena slid off me, bounced up on to her knees and swore loudly—Lena has the pottiest mouth in south London—when she scrutinized the paused image on the screen. I was red-faced and started to stutter an explanation.

'I…it's…erm—'

'What the fuck! What kind of site is this, fuck-face?'

—Lena's pet name for me.

'It's YouTube.'

'The fuck is it YouTube.'

Lena tilted her head and pointed at the screen.

'You do not see this kind of stuff on YouTube.'

'It's YouTube. Take a look.'

'I will take a look.'

She did. It was. It was YouTube.

'Fuck me. How did they get away with…this?'

'I have no idea. It's a mystery.'

The paused image on the screen that so stunned Lena was an erotic one involving Margot Kidder and another actress.

'Jesus, would you look at your gal? Margot Kidder did lesbian porn?'

'Well, it's not really lesbian porn…well… this bit…sort of is, but the rest is this weird sort of horror thing. And this is the mild bit of the scene…I don't really want to call it porn. Can we call it a tasteful and erotic love scene?'

Lena shook her head and pinched my cheeks.

'I don't really think we can. Can we? When did you find this?'

'Yesterday.'

'You mean…you've seen this already?'

'Of course.'

'Of course! What do you mean of course, you prick!'

'Well…I…I just can't believe that it's out there. It's new on me and I…'

'Arsehole. It's like your birthday and Christmas rolled into one. Your favourite gal doing—well—stuff with another gal.' Lena grimaced, shook her head. 'Christ, your sabbatical is going to be one enormous wank. So, what's this thing called?'

'Driveshaft.'

Lena snuggled up against me, under the quilt, against the headboard. '*Driveshaft*! Nice. So…is this the start?'

'No. We miss the opening credits and maybe a bit, not sure how much, of the film.'

'Go on then, roll it.'

I pointed the cursor back to the beginning of the time bar. The timer hit eleven seconds and we were away:

```
Exterior. Daytime. Panoramic shot of semi-
arid landscape (think Death Valley). Camera
is panning from right to left. Bright blue
```

sky, big yellow sun. We almost have to shield our eyes. Sand and scrub as far as the eye can see. Camera pauses on a burnt-out car. As we slowly start to move towards the car, cut to a bird's-eye view of a desert road elsewhere. A light blue Mustang with a white roof, moves into shot. Too loud engine noise on soundtrack. The car leaves a huge cloud of grit and dust and sand in its wake. The Mustang is then almost hidden by the film's title, Driveshaft, in large red capitals, which rolls—the wrong way?—from right to left across the screen. This is followed by one of the film's many blackouts.

Lena turned to me and frowned.

'What's going on? How long does it last?'

'This one, about twenty seconds. Better get used to it, Leen, there are loads of them.'

'Weird.'

'Maybe, but what is truly, and I do mean truly, weird is that I've never heard of the film. It's not on Margot's filmography, or any list anywhere. I've looked all over… believe me.'

'Oh, I believe you.'

'There were a couple of minor US TV series called *Driveshaft* and it's the name of the rock band in *Lost*. Remember *Lost*?'

Lena frowned.

'Been trying to forget it.'

'Who uploaded it?'

'Erm…'

I minimised the screen and looked at the username below.

'Erm…SB and…well his, or her, face is just a shadow.'
'Click on it.'
I did. I clicked on SB.
'No followers…no other uploads…weird.'
'Anyway, like I said…this thing, apparently, doesn't exist. It's bizarre. Fuck knows where it came from, just popped up out of the digital ether. You want to watch the rest of it?'

'After that build-up? of course I do. And, besides, have you seen the weather? I think we should postpone that walk and hibernate.'

It was raining heavily again—had been for about a week—and it was dark and cold. I changed the angle of the laptop screen and re-joined Lena again up against the headboard. Lena turned off the bedside lamp. We gathered the quilt around us, adjusted the pillows and got warm. The walk was off. *Driveshaft* was on.

I pressed play.

After the blackout, which lasts about twenty seconds, fade to an interior, black and white, shot. In the centre of this shot is Margot. (Margot Kidder plays Margot! A young woman who lives in a small town in New Mexico. There is something rotten in this small town, but we and the characters—apart from Margot it seems—are never exactly sure what it is. What we are sure of though, as the film unravels, is that Margot has some kind of gift).
We are in a grim-looking workspace which looks grimmer due to the black and white footage; cheap florescent lights, dark

walls, dark floor. Margot walks towards
the camera along this long corridor. Her
heels echo loudly. It sounds great, very
loud, atmospheric (think Lee Marvin as
Walker in *Point Blank*). The staccato echo
is now joined by howls of off-screen
laughter. Margot is in medium shot, mid-
stride, angry expression when the film
freezes.

'What the actual fuck. Is it stuck?'

'No, there's a few of these freezes throughout. Not sure if
it's our end or their end—if you know what I mean. Although,
it's stylistic, I think.'

The frozen image captures Margot head to
toe. Left foot lifted, right arm extended
forward, bent at the elbow. She looks
slightly askance of camera—left—eyes
wide, lips slightly parted. She is
clearly unhappy. She wears a tight-
fitting, just above knee-length, white
dress with darker coloured flowers—saucy
Laura Ashley. A small dark bag—possibly
leather—is tucked under her left arm. Her
figure is full and she is at the apex of
her beauty. Her face is strong but
fragile. She wears her dark hair in bangs
that almost brush the lashes of her large
eyes. The eyes are bewitching and contain
a little extra. This little extra could be
filed under one, some or all of the following:
pain, compassion, fear, prescience; call it

whatever you will but it's tough to deny
that it's there. Margot's a flower on the
dungheap of her surroundings.

'Wow, your gal looks gooooooood.'
'Yeah.'
'Better than me?'
'No way.'
'Prick.'

After a perhaps ten second 'eyeful' of
Margot, the film resumes. Margot walks a
little further towards us, opens a door
to her left and disappears. We are jarred
somewhat; left alone with just the
anonymous POV. The camera 'hangs around'
and shoots a pair of large metallic doors
at the end of the grim corridor. During
this pause, or freeze, again, maybe ten
seconds, we continue to hear the off-
screen laughter. Then a deep, crude,
gravelly, very slow, southern male voice
(think Slim Pickens) drawls sluggishly
above the laughter:

Male Voice: Maaaargot? Hey, Maaaaaaaargot,
honey.

More laughter; male, raucous.

'Hold on. Her character's name is Margot?'
'Yep.'
'That's weird. Is that weird?'

'Not really.'

We cut to Margot standing in a small bathroom, looking at herself ruefully in the mirror. We hear the loud, tormenting, slow drawl again.

Male Voice: Margot, my lap's still warm and it's waiting for your sweet little butt. Don't be shy now, honey.

More laughter.

The camera is up high and opposite the mirror in the bathroom. It's a medium close-up so we look down at the back of Margot's head and shoulders and see her face, shoulders and cleavage in the mirror. The bathroom is poorly lit. The film stock still appears to be black and white, but it can't be, as the softest orange glow hovers in and around the mirror. Tears have meant that there are two tiny, and perfectly symmetrical, mascara streams on each of Margot's cheeks. (The streams must have appeared as we were busy watching the empty corridor). Margot leans on the sink. Her face is very close to the mirror. She is sniffling. Margot spits venomously into a tissue, wipes the mascara from her cheeks and around her pain-filled eyes. She is quite meticulous. As she does this a low, throbbing electrical hum (think

fridge motor) creeps eerily on to the
soundtrack. After a few seconds there is
some more variation in the humming, and
it is accompanied by subtitles. We
realise that the sound is in fact
Margot's interior monologue.

Subtitles: Cunt man. Cunt man. Kill this
man…kill this man if he is like this
again.

Lena bolted to attention.

'Woah there! Hold your horses. So, she's a…what?—an alien? and two C bombs within the first line!'

'Guess so. Strong stuff, no?'

'I'll say. Only in the 70s. Love it.'

Margot is re-applying mascara to her left
eye. She is still sniffling. She moves
back slightly from the mirror and pauses,
pouts slightly, scrutinizing her 'brushwork'.
The image freezes again: Margot poised, ready
to apply mascara to her right eyelashes,
brush in right hand, mouth open. It is a
striking image. The left eye is already
heavily mascaraed—too heavily perhaps
(think Alex and his droogs from *A
Clockwork Orange*).

'What the fuck!'

'Yeah.'

'Weird.'

'Yeah?'

'She looks like one of that gang from that…oh, what's it called, that horrible film they banned…oh …'

Lena stumbled on.

'… oh, you know with the fish-faced guy…oh what's his fucking name…erm, Malcolm McDonald…oh what's it fucking called?'

'Clockwork Orange?'

'That's it.'

'Malcolm McDowell?'

'That's him. You kept me dangling—'

Lena delivered each syllable with a punch.

'Like. a. Fish. on. a. Fuck. ing. Hook.'

'Ouch! Leen, you cow, that really fucking hurt.'

'So, is that a—what do you call it?—tribute or homage or something to Clockwork Orange? I mean…it seems to be. Who directed it?'

'No idea. No credits. No info. Remember?'

'Yeah.'

    Margot 'unfreezes' and carefully continues
    to make up her right eye. The throbbing,
    electrical hum returns along with the
    subtitles.

    Subtitles: Cunt man is a creep man is a
    bad man. How can…how can he? when he knows?
    The thought of this man…of this man makes
    me hurt so much inside.

    Margot applies lipstick now. Slowly and
    carefully. Erotically? She puckers up,
    aims a somewhat incongruous kiss (She

seems to have recovered) at herself? us?
the mirror? The laughter, which we can
now hear more clearly, is accompanied by
animal noises, nasty, guttural sounds.
Margot sneers. Puts her make-up away in
her small black bag. Echoing footsteps,
loud and quick, now wander on to the
soundtrack and the other noises diminish.
We stay in the bathroom with Margot. The
footsteps stop outside the bathroom door.
There is a momentary beat of silence
before we hear—loudly—a match being
struck. Margot turns to the toilet door.
We see her side profile in the mirror.
She bites her bottom lip during the
following exchange. We're yet to see who
owns the other voice.

Beacham: You all right in there, Margot?
Margot: Yeah, I'm okay, Beacham. Thanks.
Beacham: Look, he was only...I know he's
a...but...
Margot: Just leemealone, Beacham. Leave
me be, please.
Beacham: All right, all right. I'm just
tryin'a...

Long Pause. Margot looking anxious and
now full beam at the mirror continues to
bite her bottom lip.

Beacham: Can I...you wanna lift home?
Margot: No. No thank you, Beacham.

Beacham: Okay…suit yerself…just…take it easy. See ya tommorra.

Margot continues to look into the mirror as Beacham's footsteps echo, then fade. The electrical hum which has never gone away, just muffled by other noises, is noticeable again. It slowly becomes louder and works in tandem with the camera which zooms slowly into the mirror. We stop at extreme close-up of Margot. We are too close and the hum is too loud.

Subtitles: Good man. A good man. Beacham is a good man.

Margot continues to stare intently at herself, lost and vulnerable and otherworldly (think David Bowie in *The Man who Fell to Earth*).
Cut—sudden and perhaps disconcerting—to exterior and back to colour. The electrical hum stops suddenly, along with the cut. The building that we presume Margot, Beacham and the off-screen characters, occupy, fills the frame. The building seems to be in the middle of nowhere. The camera is still for maybe twenty seconds before it slowly zooms out to reveal semi-arid landscape either side of the building. Relentless blue sky above. The building is a one-storey structure with a flat roof, metallic window-frames and doors. The windows are

large and blacked out and the four of
them, two either side, are split by the
metallic double-doors. There are two
large satellite dishes, back to back,
that point off left and off right. Two
cars are parked in the tiny make-shift
car park. Then a third car, a brown sedan,
reverses into, and then drives, out of
shot. We presume that this is Beacham and
can just spot his white Stetson hat and
bushy, salt and pepper beard before he
drives away.
The camera is still; nerveless-ly still,
again. Nothing happens for almost half a
minute. We just see the building in
medium shot. Nothing on the soundtrack at
all; not even—as we might expect—the
squawk of a bird or the sound of the wind.

'What the fuck! Is this some kind of art-house film?'
'Not sure.'
'Will you move, you fucker.'
'Me?'
'No, this fucker.'
Lena is about to move the film along when the action
resumes.

Loud, echoing footsteps interrupt the
silence. They stop as we continue to
watch the building. Then the footsteps
resume. Margot exits the building, out of
the left-hand door. The door squeaks as
she opens and closes it. It's bright and

Margot has to shade her eyes from the sun. She is smoking a cigarette. Now the filmstock is colour we can see Margot's tasteful dress is sprinkled generously with small red flowers (hard to make out but perhaps morning glory).
The camera pans slowly from right to left across the barren landscape. Cut back to medium close-up of Margot.

Margot: (As if practising elocution.) How are you, New Mexico? (Takes deep draw on cigarette. The smoke drifts from her mouth as she speaks). How are you? How are ya? How are ya – ya – ya – ya. Hey, how are ya?

Cut back to landscape. Apart from sand and rocks there are cacti, some sorry looking grassy clumps and two apparently abandoned cars—not the ones in the car park. Cut back to Margot in mid-close-up who draws deep and long on her cigarette, as if she is practising smoking. She takes three further slow and sumptuous draws, and slowly lets the smoke just drift from her mouth. It takes a good minute or so. Margot—the actress—does a decent job. She hardly blinks. We see a kind of magic in her eyes—the 'extra' again, mentioned above. After the final sumptuous pull, Margot drops the cigarette. Cut to close-up of black heel swivelling on the butt. Erotic? Cut back to Margot in medium

shot. She opens the metallic door nearest
her. It squeaks. The camera moves past
her, through the door and into the
building. The black and white footage
resumes, as does the electrical hum.

Subtitles: Blood to the cunt man. Bring
the blood to the cunt man.

'What the fuck was that? I've never seen that. A character
opens the door for the camera! That is just weird. More arty
shit?'
'Yeah? Dunno. Maybe.'

Interior: the camera enters the building
and moves slowly, unsteadily down the
corridor (it's a slow uncomfortable ride,
not least because we don't know who we're
accompanying). There is a door at the other
end of the corridor with a frosted glass
panel. The camera pauses. We half expect
a knock. The door opens. We are not sure
who opens it. Again, the camera is still
as it shoots a fat, besuited man in medium
shot. Before him is a large dark telephone,
a coffee cup and papers strewn across the
table—some splattered with a dark liquid.
Blood? Behind him is a large filing
cabinet with a coffee pot on top. Behind
that is a high window which shows us half
barren landscape and half cloudless sky.
The man leans back in a chair, holding
his nose with a tissue, looking up

towards the ceiling. He breathes heavily
and groans. He has a bad nosebleed. There
is a large bloodstain on his shirt. His
necktie is hanging over his left
shoulder. The camera lingers.

'Holy fuck, nosebleeds, not nosebleeds.'
'You don't like them?'
'Like them. Who the fuck likes them?'

Blackout.

Fade to Margot and her lover kissing
passionately in a dark, candle-lit bedroom.

'What the fuck! One minute we're…Woah, is she actually
going to…is she?…she is. My god!'
'Yeah.'
'What the fuck kind of film is this? She's not going to…holy
fuck…she is too. I didn't know it was this bad.'
'Bad?'
'Christ on a scooter!'

Margot and her lover swap places.

'Woah, what?…how long does this last?'
'Two, three minutes. We can time it.'
'Again —I've got to ask—how in the fuck did they get away
with uploading this? Or even making it in the first place?'
'Don't know. Like I said, I think it's been found in a dusty
vault somewhere and…hey presto.'
Lena's eyes were enormous.

'Shall I skip it?' I asked.
'Erm.'
Lena didn't want me to skip it.

The sauce comes to an end. The post-coital scene is beautifully lit and clearly choreographed. The camera hovers above Margot and her lover, Eve, as they smoke. We see the two actresses in semi-silhouette; bare shoulders and beautiful faces. The lovers look up towards us—but not at us. The conversation is stilted. They both sound rather flat but their tender intimacy conveys a deep affection. Candlelight flickers around the room.

Margot: Any juice?
Eve: No, baby. Not since I been here anyway.
Margot: How was Ringo's?
Eve: Okay…till bout quarter of two when we lost the juice.
Margot: Pretzels and potato chips?
Eve: Yep…and beer. Though that soon got warm.

The two lovers carry on smoking. They blow the bluish smoke up towards the camera. The smoke hangs in the dim, flickering candlelight. Eve and Margot turn to their bedside table ashtrays simultaneously. They put out their cigarettes. They ease back on to their

pillows and face one another. We get a
little closer. For some reason their
voices are even quieter.

Eve: Same shit at work?
Margot: Yep…same shit.
Eve: What you gonna do?
Margot: Don't know.

Eve moves even closer to Margot. Kisses
her softly on the cheek. Margot turns her
head to look back up towards—but not at—
us. Eve whispers in her ear. We can just
about make out what she is saying. Eve
puts strong and equal emphasis on all
three syllables.

Eve: Yes…you…do.

Margot's expression doesn't change or
perhaps there is the tiniest flicker of
her left eye. Eve then turns back to look
up towards—but not at—the camera, seems
to speak to us.

Eve: Yes…you…do.

Slow, slow fade, from the beautiful faces
in the smoky, blue haze to Beacham
driving along in the dark. The windscreen
fills the frame so that we see his face
in medium close-up. He appears happy. He
scratches his salt and pepper beard,
adjusts his white Stetson. Cut to

headlights on the desert road. The car
eats up the white lines. We cut back and
forth between the illuminated road and
Beacham's face in medium close-up. Each
time Beacham appears to be less happy,
something seems to be slowly creeping up
on him. He half closes his eyes, first as
if he is in deep thought, then confusion,
then pain. The low electrical hum slowly
hovers on to the soundtrack. The next
time we cut back to Beacham his nose is
bleeding heavily.

Subtitles: Blood to the sweet man.

Beacham: What the fuck?

Beacham slows the car, pulls to the side
of the road, in front of the camera. He
takes off his Stetson. He starts to wipe
his bloody nose with a handkerchief. Cut
to Beacham looking down at blood-
spattered shirt.

Beacham: What the fuck!

'No…more…nosebleeds. Why? Can you pause it? I need a pee.'
'Sure.'
I pressed pause.
'Want a beer?'
'Sure.'

The film was paused on Beacham's face. I was trying to place the actor but was struggling. Lena came back with two cans of beer. She studied Beacham's face too.

'Who is he?'

'I've no idea.'

'Oh, hold on…I know…isn't that…oh, you know…the guy from…oh, shit, what's it called…you know that boxing movie with that other guy, you know, the one you like…you know, he's from that acting dynasty…oh, shit…it's coming, it's coming…Bridges…the Bridges…Jeff Bridges.'

'That's not Jeff Bridges.'

'I know that, fuck face. I mean, the other guy who's in that boxing film with him…with Jeff Bridges.'

'Oh…I've got it…*Fat City*…Stacy Keach.'

I looked closer. Tilted and then shook my head.

'No. No way.'

'You sure? Google it…or IMDB it…or whatever.'

'No. Firstly, it's not him and secondly…if it was him, this film isn't anywhere on Margot Kidder's CV so why would it be on Stacy Keach's?'

'Fuck knows. It's your mystery.'

'It is weird though.'

'What?'

'Well, now that you come to mention it, I don't recognise anybody else in the whole film.'

'So…you can't know every actor from the 70s.'

'No, but I know most of them, American ones, anyhow, and apart from Margot I don't recognise anybody.'

'Weird?'

'Potentially.'

'Shit. Hailstones, sounds like a fucking machine gun.'

Lena and I bounced up off the bed, peered through the curtains like excited kids, heads touching, noses on the window-pane.

'Check it out,' said Lena. 'It's the apocalypse.'

'Yeah, I think Noah's on the way.'

It was hard to see much of the street because of the curtain of hail. I could make out the red and white blur of car lights coming and going, and the fuzzy white of the streetlights. There was also a low orange glow which seemed to be throbbing from the local supermarket.

We returned to bed, snuggled up, snapped open our beers, touched cans.

> We are back to Beacham in mid-close-up. He stands in front of his car still attending to his bloody nose. The headlights seem to shine through him and his pale suit. He starts to cough. He inspects the blood-soaked handkerchief, then scrunches it into his jacket pocket. Beacham stumbles back on to the hood of his car. He looks up with a puzzled expression. A heavy but quiet mechanical whir slowly gets louder as we focus on the beleaguered looking Beacham. Initially, we figure it's the low electrical hum again, but this is different. The mechanical whir gets louder. It soon becomes obvious that it is the sound of a helicopter. Beacham looks up as the helicopter circles above him. A white and blue chopper with a blue light.

Beacham: What the fuck?

Cut to high shot as we see helicopter's blue light circle Beacham and his car. He staggers forward and shields his eyes from the blue light. The blades create a powerful wind that blows Beacham's Stetson from his head. His salt-and-pepper hair is long and flies everywhere. Cut to Beacham as he watches the phantom chopper fly up and out of shot.

Beacham: What the fuck?

Cut to back of Beacham in medium shot, staggering back to his car. He stops, shuffles out into the dark, and out of shot. We presume he is looking for his Stetson. The camera stays on the stationary car as we hear Beacham, grunting, groaning, cussing. He is gone for about half a minute, and just as we might have started to think that he might not return, he does. He stumbles back into shot wearing his Stetson and cussing. The helicopter noise is just discernible. As Beacham gets into the driver's seat the headlights blink off. The screen goes black. We only hear what goes on.

'Fuck me. They could have lit it.'
'I like it. It's a nice touch, I think. What you would see in the middle of the desert when It's pitch black anyway?'

'Loads. Stars? Starlight? Moon?'

'I don't know. Maybe it's another deliberate blackout.'

Beacham is turning over the engine. He is swearing as the engine keeps stalling. We hear him pounding the dashboard and cussing some more. Then turning the key in the ignition again, to no avail.

Beacham: What the fuck?

(Beacham's 'what the fuck?' almost leaks into the following scene.) Fade to Margot and Eve in their candle-lit room. The couple are just getting out of bed. (The beautiful lighting and choreographed movement is still in evidence—more so.) Margot and Eve exit either side of the bed which is dead centre of shot. Both are naked and walk towards us, semi-silhouetted in the candle-light—it's tough to argue that this is not extremely gratuitous (not one for the feminists). Margot and Eve are almost atop the camera, their pubes bearing down on the viewer when the lights suddenly come on. Cut to view of kitchen which adjoins the bedroom. The kitchen is small, tidy, and very brightly lit.

Margot: Juice. Move. Quick.

The camera is—once again—stationary during the following scene. We see what unfolds from a comfortable distance, as

if we are sat on the bed. Although the scene could be construed as comical—owing mostly to the speed at which the actresses move and their nudity—the intensity of their actions and their serious facial expressions probably invalidate any laughs.
Margot flings open the fridge door. Close-up on Margot's excited face for a beat. Eve slams opens cupboards. Takes out cans. Close-up on Eve's excited face for a beat. It becomes clear that the lovers are gathering food in order to cook it while the 'juice' is on. Margot turn on the oven and flings in something that looks like pizza. Eve is busy chopping vegetables. Margot puts the kettle on to the stove. The lovers yelp with glee as the blue flame bursts violently into life. Close up of the warming kettle atop blue flame for a couple of beats. Zoom out to Margot and Eve chopping in unison. They fill a pan. They both turn to look at the kettle. Waiting for the whistle. Suddenly, Eve bolts out of shot.

Margot: What?
Eve (Off-camera): Shower.
Margot: Shit.

Margot bolts out of shot. We zoom in on the kettle on the stove for a couple of beats. Cut, predictably perhaps, to the

two women sharing a shower. The scene,
though, does not turn into a gratuitous
romp—which we may have been expecting
owing to earlier sections. The women are
obviously relieved. And the only noises
are to do with relief and satisfaction at
the hot water that cascades over them. In
the shower the camera is above the fixed
showerhead (think *Psycho*) and we see the
women from the top of their heads on
down. The sharp whistling of the kettle
slowly drowns out the soft sound of the
shower.
Cut to the women standing in the kitchen,
wolfing down the food. Cut to them,
medium close up, at a small table staring
intensely at one another, smiling,
laughing, in love. Cut to them lighting
candles as 'juice' seems to have gone off
again. Cut to them standing in front yard
under a huge moon. Cut to them smoking in
bed. They kiss. The lights go out.

Blackout.

'What's the rush? I don't get it. Cut, cut, cut. Don't get a
chance to know the other one…what's her name?'
'Eve.'
'Yeah, Eve. Who's Eve. Do you recognise her?'
Eve has long dirty blonde hair with sparkling green eyes.
Facially, she resembles Dee Wallace who turned up in a few cult
horror films in the late 70s and early 80s (most notably *The Hills
Have Eyes* and *The Howling*) but was best known as the mom in

ET. But Eve isn't Dee Wallace. I do not know who she is. Nor Beacham. Nor the fat man in the office—although it wasn't easy to see his face.

'No.'

Lena looks thoughtful and towards the window and the sound of the heavy rain hidden by the curtains.

'Well, sometimes you get directors who use amateurs or less knowns. You know, like that lefty bloke…the Brit…you know…the old guy…oh, shit…did that one about the Irish…did that one about the Spanish…oh, fuck… did Cathy, go home, what's his name?'

'*Kathy Come Home.* Ken Loach.'

'Ken Loach.'

'Yeah but why have an amateur cast alongside a professional actor. I mean Margot can act, right?'

'I dunno…like I say, your mystery, mate.'

```
During blackout we hear coughing and
swearing. For a long moment, this might
well grate as these noises do not
'square' with the nubile young women, we
have just shared time and space with.
Fade to close-up of Beacham in his car.
He is reclining his seat and swaddling
himself in a blanket. He has on the
overhead light.

Beacham: What a fuckin' day, lord: fuckin'
nosebleed, fuckin' spy-chopper, fuckin'
dead car. What have I done to deserve all
this attention, lord?
```

Beacham fidgets. Tries to get comfortable. Reclines, un-reclines, etc.

Beacham: Gonna freeze to death or be cougar meat. Fuck. Keep an eye on me please, lord. I been bad, but there's plenty been much worse than me. I could rattle some names off to ya, if it'll help my case, but I ain't that kind. Tell ya what, lord…help me make it through the night, promise I'll see ya at chapel on Sunday. Deal?

Beacham turns off the overhead light.

Blackout.

During this blackout the volume slowly increases to 'reveal' sounds of upset and agitation; screaming, shouting, swearing. The disturbing noises seem to fill the darkness to bursting point. Slow fade to Margot back in the workplace toilet. The camera is behind her once more so that we see her head and shoulders and cleavage in the mirror. The orange glow seems more pronounced now. Margot is weeping and shuddering. Leaning on the sink, looking down, shaking her head. We hear Eve's phrase from last night, echo about the bathroom, as Margot's interior monologue:

Yes…you…do. Yes…you…do.

Now, footsteps, loud and quick and echoing, move in on Margot. Margot turns to the door. Resumes her lip biting. There is a knock on the door. Margot opens her mouth but, nothing comes out. The knocking on the toilet door becomes loud, rhythmical. The exchange that follows is whispered. Some of it is almost drowned out by the distressed voices which switch between background and foreground on the soundtrack. The camera stays in the bathroom with Margot and her distress.

Beacham: Margot? Margot, you in there?
Margot: Beacham?
Beacham: What the hell, girl!
Margot: Beacham…I …
Beacham: Oh, my Lord…what the fuck, girl!
Margot: Beacham…I didn't touch him.
Beacham (loud): Oh, my Lord…
Margot: I didn't touch him, Beacham.
Beacham (louder): Oh my—
Margot: Beacham?
Prolonged and heavy silence.
Margot (loud, panicking): Beacham?
Beacham: Shit, girl, I—
Margot: Can you get me outta here?

There is a long pause. Panicking footsteps like sporadic tap-dancing, echo on to the soundtrack. The camera stays with Margot who looks more and more anxious during the following exchanges. She bites her bottom lip. Stares at the door. Winces every now and then.

Eileen: Beach…Beach, oh my Lord, what we gonna do? Have ya seen what someone did to him, Beach? Who could do that, Beach?
Jack: Eileen…. Eileen. Hold it there, hun.
Eileen: Did you…did you see him…what's left of him back there? It's a curse, Beach. Oh, my Lord. I knew somethin' like this was brewing. I could feel it. Tell him, Jack.
Jack: Calm down, hun. I'm gonna…go get Sheriff Beale, Beach. He ain't answering his radio but he's out there on the road somewhere. Gotta be.
Beacham (Confusion and hesitancy in his voice): Okay…okay, Jack, that's a…a good idea.
Eileen: Jack, hunny, no, that ain't a good idea. Probly the Sheriff's car is broke like all the rest of em. It's a curse, Beach. Oh my Lord, Beach…it's a curse.
Jack: Well, my vehicle is okay. I'm gonna go find Sheriff Beale. He needs ta know bout this. We caint jus' leave him…like…like that…back there…like that. Taint Christian.
Eileen: Wait, don't leave me here, Jack. I don't wanna be here no more. I'm coming. You coming, Beach?

Beacham: I...I'll be along, Eileen. I'll try the radio again. You go along. I'll be along.
Eileen: Suit yerself...but don't stay round here...it's cursed, Beach, I'm tellin' ya.

The footsteps fade into the distance. We hear the double-doors squeak open and close.

Beacham: Margot. As I live and breathe, girl, what...

Margot's hand moves towards the handle of the bathroom door. Cut to medium shot. Camera on corridor. We see Beacham, pacing outside the bathroom door. Margot suddenly stumbles into shot and into Beacham's arms. Close-up on Beacham's worried expression.

Margot (voice muffled, weeping into Beacham's chest): Help me Beacham. Please help me. I didn't wanna...honest I didn't wanna but it was getting bad. He was making it so tough for me and Eve. You don't know, Beacham, you just don't know.

Beacham looks concerned and back towards the double doors.

Beacham: Margot...we have ta get outta here, right now...okay.

The camera stays where it is and we watch
Beacham and Margot trot, hand in hand,
towards the double doors. Beacham leads the
way out into the sun which momentarily
floods most of the corridor with light.
The doors squeak open and closed. The
camera lingers in the bleak black and white
of the work-place corridor whilst the
characters are outside. Another uncomfortable
moment as we feel trapped in black and white
with something potentially extremely
unpleasant close by.

'Fuck. Get on with it. Is it frozen again or what? This guy
knows how to kill it.'
'He?'
'Okay, whoever. Can't you move it forward?'

The camera makes a 180-degree turn and
heads back towards the frosted glass
office door, slowly. When it finally gets
to the door it pauses. We may well be
waiting for the door to swing open and
reveal the apparent horror that awaits
but…

Blackout.

'What the fuck? What…why can't we see…we all want to
see it, don't we? Why be so fucking…what's the word…you
know?'
'Tantalising?'
'No, you know…oh, what is it? Erm…'

'Postmodern?'

'No…hold on, it's coming…twattish, that's it. Why be such a twat? We all want to see the fucking gore. Why rob us of the pleasure of seeing it?'

'Well, they—he, she—is leaving it up to you, the viewer. Is that not okay?'

'No, it's fucking petulance. Has to be a bloke who made this. That's about power. He's saying, I could show it but I'm going to withhold. He's probably a premature ejaculator.'

'Ouch.'

'Just give us the fucking gore.'

```
Fade to exterior, wide-shot. We are back
to colour and on a desert road. Late
morning sun, huge, very bright, very
high. A car is moving towards us. It's
Beacham's brown sedan. It shimmers in the
intense heat. A substantial cloud of dust
billows behind the vehicle. We wait for
the car to get closer. The wait is
interminable. We may start to wonder
whether the car is actually moving. Cut
to medium close-up. We see Margot and
Beacham through the windscreen. Margot
bites her lip. She looks lost, eyes huge
and elsewhere. Beacham is adjusting his
Stetson. He looks perturbed. Beacham
gestures as if he is about to say
something but changes his mind. He clears
his throat.

Beacham: So, where we goin'?
Margot: I…I don't know yet, Beacham.
```

There is a long pause. Cut to bird's-eye shot above car. We see the car heading into the sand. Cut back to 'windscreen' shot. Margot sits up and looks as if she has just remembered something.

Margot: The highway.
Beacham: What? The sixty-six?
Margot: Yeah…the sixty-six.Can you do that, Beacham? Can you take me on the sixty-six? Drop me there?
Beacham: There! Where? It's the longest god-damned road in the country.
Margot: Sokay, I know where.
Beacham: Okay, sure…but…who's gonna pick ya up?
Margot: Beacham, you wanna help me or—
Beacham: Of course, I do but…

Beacham turns to Margot. Again, he is about to say something but changes his mind. He does this a number of times until the effect is almost comical. Margot, meantime, leans her head on the passenger door window, bites her lip. Eventually, Beacham speaks.

Beacham: Oh, fuck it, I gotta ask. So tell me…how did you do…how…that…thing…I mean…you know to make somebody end up…like that…like him?

Beacham clears his throat. Margot turns
slowly to Beacham.

Margot (in a lifeless whisper): I didn't
touch him, Beacham.
Beacham: Okay…I know you didn't…touch
him, but—
Margot (louder, more insistent): I didn't
touch him.

There is a long and uncomfortable pause.
It's obvious that Beacham wants to push
but stops himself.

Beacham: I'm sorry. But, Lord, you've
left a hell of a mess, girl.

Beacham's look towards Margot is pure
paternal affection, almost canine; sad
eyes, down-turned mouth. Margot leans
against the passenger window again.
Closes her eyes and replays—for us!—what
happened an hour or so ago.
Flashback. Interior. Back to black and
white. We follow Margot as she walks
along the corridor. The camera is close
and shaky. Hand-held.

'Wow! That's …I don't know, quite innovative, isn't it? For
the time?'

'Maybe, pretty uncommon for the era, I guess.'

'Bit like that bloke, the one you like…oh, what's his name?
does lots of hand-held stuff, did that horrible skinhead film with

that actor, that English actor who did stuff in Hollywood. Oh fuck, you know he did some Tarantino films. Oh, who am I on about?'

'Alan Clarke, Tim Roth. *Made in Britain*?'

'Nobody like a smartass.'

    Margot's heels click-clack and echo along
    the corridor. The electrical hum slowly
    throbs its way on to the soundtrack.
    Margot walks towards the door with the
    frosted glass panel. We hear soft voices
    and laughter behind the door. Cut to
    close-up of Margot. Her eyes are closed.
    The electrical hum gets louder. Margot
    stops before the door.

    Subtitles: Time is now, time is now. Cunt
    man must die… must die. Cunt man must
    die.
    We hear coughing on the other side of the
    door—just below the hum. Cut to extreme
    close-up of Margot. Eyes still closed.
    Cut to close-up of Margot's hands on the
    frosted glass of the door. Her fingers
    slowly spread. The coughing gets louder.
    So does the humming.

    Subtitles: Close now, closer now. Cunt
    man is dying, is dying. Cunt man is
    dying.

    Cut back to Margot and her closed eyes.
    The coughing is accompanied by gasps.

Loud and desperate. We hear a collage of confused, panicking noise below the coughing and the gasping and now the choking. Cut to close up of Margot's face. Her eyes suddenly open, extremely wide. Loud scream from behind the door.

Blackout.

Fade to Beacham and Margot in mid-shot through the windscreen again. They could have been driving forever. Margot is jerked out of her reverie by Beacham's loud voice. He is strangely—considering circumstances—chirpy. Perhaps he is trying to cheer Margot.

Beacham: (Looking up at the sky out of the windscreen, laughs to himself): You know what happened to me last night? Right about here?

Margot tries to stir herself.

Margot: What?
Beacham: I said, you know what happened to me last night? Right around here?

Margot sits up, rubs her eyes.

Margot: No…what?
Beacham: Well, I'll tell ya, since you're askin'. First off, I gotta another one of

them nosebleeds. Seem to be fuckin'
contagious. Can they be?
Margot: I don't know what you mean.

Beacham's sidelong glance at Margot
contains a shadow of suspicion.

Beacham: Anyway, I pull over, get out the
car to clean myself—the blood—and, well,
next thing this chopper circles right the
fuck above me. Bright blue light fucking
blindin' me…bout ten feet or so above my
head. Prob'ly taking pictures or some
such. Blew my hat clean off my fuckin'
head. You believe that? think I'm making
that up?

Margot almost smiles.

Margot: They do lots of shitty military
stuff round here, Beacham. You know that.
Beacham: Yeah, I know that. But…why would
they—whoever they are—bother with a poor
sap like me?
Margot: I dunno, Beacham…maybe they liked
your hat.
Beacham: Hey, a joke. Anyway, guess what
happens next?
Margot: What?
Beacham: The fucking car breaks down. And
correct me if I'm wrong but that is also
becoming contagious. Am I right?

Margot frowns. Beacham grimaces.

Beacham: Fuck, now what's this?
Margot: You okay?
Beacham: Nope…I got them pins and needles again. That's another sunbitching, freaking goddamn regular occurrence round here too. What…argh! It's killin'.

Beacham starts hitting his legs with one hand.

Beacham: Shit, it's spreading right up…up my legs. What the fuck!

Beacham grimaces. Pounds his legs. Cut to bird's-eye view as car zigzags, on and off the road.

Margot: Beacham, what the fuck? Pull over, you're gonna kill us.
Beacham: My legs. It's spreadin'…I caint feel em.

The car eases off the road. Comes to a standstill. We view the car from on high. The shot freezes.

Blackout.

During the blackout—longer than usual, just under thirty seconds—we hear a loud thud, then silence, then the wind; from quiet to loud whisper. The fade is slow, from black to blinding brightness. Medium shot of the front of Beacham's car. Sand

is being whipped up around the car.
Camera slowly moves into 'windscreen'
shot and eerie tableaux. Margot stares
vacantly ahead, left eye twitching.
Beacham lies back, head on the headrest
at an angle, blood running from his nose.
Much of his beard is stained red. His
eyes are open. His Stetson is just about
on his head, held on by the headrest. It
feels as if a long time has passed.
Camera is still as Margot exits the
passenger door, walks around the front of
the car. Stops at the driver's side. She
takes Beacham's hat from his head through
the open window. She places it on her
head. She takes a few steps away from the
car and pauses. She walks back and closes
Beacham's eyes, kisses his forehead.

'Woah…hold on. Stop right there. 'What? What? What? Why? Why? Why would she kill him? I mean the fat guy, her boss or whoever, I get, but poor old Beacham. He has only been good to her. I don't get it.'

'I don't know, maybe she didn't kill him or she's an alien under orders to bump off as many humans as possible? I don't really care. I'm sort of enjoying the ride, you know.'

'No, I don't know. I think I want to get off. I hate it when they bump off nice characters and leave the assholes.'

Margot: So long, Beacham. And thanks.

Margot looks out at what awaits her: a huge expanse of sand, red rocks in the distance, sun is bright and huge and low in the unreal blue. Cut to close up of Margot. Sand flies into her face. She spits and closes her eyes. She holds on to the Stetson. The camera pans around to the right and we see an abandoned car. Cut back to Margot. She acknowledges car. Narrows her eyes. Cut to wide shot. Margot walks towards the car. Cut to car interior, Margot searches back and front. Hand under seats. Cut to close-up of Margot's face. She's found something. Smiles. Cut to medium-shot of Margot's back. She is carrying a water canteen with the strap over her shoulder. Looks like it's from an old Western; brown, worn leather. Margot pauses to take off her shoes. She flings them out of shot and we hear two soft, off-screen, thuds. She then eases into what can only be described as a catwalk wiggle—arguably, considering the circumstances, the most incongruous walk available. Margot's sultry saunter into desert and the huge yellow sun is accompanied by the electrical hum which, again, slowly creeps up on us.

Subtitles: Fireball hurt. Fireball danger. Hot. Slow, slow to the fireball.

We track Margot's progress, in her
sashaying white dress—plain white, loose
fit—and matching Stetson and brown
leather water bottle over her left
shoulder, for almost a minute as she
wanders away from us into the shimmering
desert heat.

Blackout.

'Should be called B*lackou*t, not *Driveshaft*. Landscape reminds me of *Planet of the Apes* or that other one…oh, shit…what's it called? Sci-fi. They think they're on the moon but they're not…got the murderer…American footballer…'

'*Capricorn One*. And OJ Simpson was found not guilty. So, you cannot call him a murderer.'

'Yeah, but come on.'

'Lena!'

'Okay, I'm sorry. Anyway, the landscape reminds me of that.'

'Lots of films are shot in deserts. Great setting for drama.'

'You call this is a drama?'

As Lena said this the rain got even heavier.

'Now that, out there, is a drama.'

'Yep, it's proper *Twilight Zone*.'

Lena did the creepy, catchy *Twilight Zone* intro.

'Fuck, of course, that's why it's not really grabbing me.'

'Why?'

'No music. This thing has no music—so far anyway. Well, unless you count that annoying fucking buzzing.'

'Humming'.

'Buzzing.'

'Humming.'
'Buzzing.'
'Humming.'
This went on for quite a time.

> Blackout for about twenty seconds. During
> this blackout we hear a car engine
> gradually getting louder. Fade to
> overhead shot of a car speeding along a
> desert road. It is the blue Mustang with
> the white roof from the opening sequence.
> The Mustang is moving away from us. At
> speed. Leaving a huge dust cloud in its
> wake. It's a high shot, perfectly framed.
> Just before the car flies out of the
> shot, cut to close-up of a woman's face.
> She is the car's driver. She is blonde,
> attractive, middle-aged and terrified.
> Cut back to overhead shot. Car flies out
> of shot.

'Who the? What the?'
'Thought you said it didn't grab you.'

> Cut to Margot. Long-shot. Walking towards
> the camera now. (Nice mirroring of previous
> walk away from us). She is still walking
> her catwalk walk. She takes a last gulp
> of water, throws the canteen over her
> shoulder.
> Cut to the terrified woman. Looking even
> more terrified. Cut to her point of view.

We see the speedometer slide past 100 mph and keep climbing. Cross-cuts between increasingly terrified expression and increasing speed. The woman starts to scream. Speedometer hits maximum 140 mph. Engine noise too loud. Drowns out woman's scream.
Cut to close-up of Margot. She takes off Stetson, wipes her sweating brow with white sleeve of her dress. She looks unperturbed, determined and replaces hat as she narrows her eyes. Cut to long-shot, we see that she is close to rocks. Cut to terrified woman's face. She is pinned back in her seat. Eyes wide. Engine sound too loud.
Cut to long-shot of back of Margot climbing the rocks. She is about half-way up. Remember she is barefoot. Cut to bird's-eye view of the blue and white Mustang which now takes in Margot finishing her climb at the top of the rocks. The blue and white Mustang is speeding towards her. Margot runs towards the car, waves the white Stetson vigorously. It seems that there is no way that the car can slow down. We are convinced it's going to hit her. But it suddenly screeches to a halt. The car throws up grit, sand, dust. It does a 360-degree turn and stops. It is an impressive stunt. The car sits and throbs and waits.

'Fuck. This is bad news. Hitchhiking never goes well in the movies. Your gal is in trouble, I'd say.'

'Looks that way.'

'And what's with that woman?'

'I don't know.'

'Pause it. I need another pee.'

Lena jumped off the bed, exited the bedroom, then poked her head back in.

'Beer?'

'Sure.'

I began to study the features of the woman in the car whose face was taking up most of the right half of the screen.

Lena returned with the beers.

'Recognise her?'

'Nope. Never seen her before in my life.'

'Hold on…isn't she…'

'Please don't.'

Lena laughed, jumped on the bed with the cans of beer. We got warm again and stared at the paused shot.

Lena tilted her head.

'I mean, it's tasteful, no? I mean, that is a well thought out shot, no? Look, you've got the fear on that actress's face…you've got poor old Margot, who is obviously fucked, innocently heading towards her doom…the tension is there…and that is so—I don't know—nicely framed? that shot? Look at it. It's almost bloody perfect.'

'Yep. No mug made this.'

'For sure.'

We touched our beer cans.

Margot watches the Stetson blow away towards the rocks. Cut to the back of the throbbing car. Cut to front of car and the terrified woman looking in her rear-view mirror.

Terrified Woman: Come on, bitch. What the fuck are you doing?

Cut to close-up of a thoughtful Margot. The throbbing hum emerges slowly on to the soundtrack. The hum is more erratic than before. A spanner is in the works, it seems. Margot frowns as the subtitles appear below her static form.

Subtitles: No...no good, no...da...dan...dang...no... Margot shakes her head and walks towards the car.

The camera shoots through the passenger window. We see the side profile of the woman and Margot's face as she leans in the driver's open window. The woman has a mark on the right-hand-side of her neck

which we see her cover with her long
blonde hair.

'Oh, no.'
Lena started to punch the quilt.
'Fucking vampires. Oh, give me a break. Not fucking
vampires.'

    Margot (Breathless): Oh, God...thank you...you
    saved my life. Thank you so much. I didn't
    think...any cars were working. They all seem
    to be broken down. Thought I was a gonna
    for sure.

    Margot notices the desperation on the
    woman's face.

    Hey...are you okay?

    Throughout the following exchange the
    woman appears to be in discomfort. She is
    grimacing, is breathless and appears
    pinned into her seat by the seatbelt.

    Woman: (Breathing heavily) Yes, I'm
    okay...I'm sorry but...I really need...help.
    Would you please help me...please?
    Margot: Sure,...sure. What do you want me
    to do?
    Woman: (Breathing heavily) Okay, look,
    I...I...I'll give you a lift but you have
    to...I need you to...please...would you please
    drive?

Margot (Frowning): Sure, that's…that's fine. You wanna move along?
Woman: (Trying to sound calmer, trying to smile) Sure. Just…can you do me one favour first? Can you get something outta the…outta the trunk for me? It's a sweater. I…you know it's…it's gonna be dark and cold real soon.

'Don't do it, Margot. Don't do it you dumb bitch.'

Margot: Sure. Is it unlocked?
Woman: Yep, should be.

Cut to close-up of nervous-looking woman. She looks in her rear-view mirror as Margot arrives at trunk. Again, we see her through both the windscreens. The trunk obscures Margot as she lifts it. And as soon as she lifts it the woman's seatbelt unbuckles automatically with a violent snap. The woman holds her leg as she shifts along into the passenger seat.

Cut. Close-up to a number of deep puncture wounds between the woman's calves and ankles. Camera pans to show bloodstains on seat and in driver's well. The woman covers her leg with her long skirt. Cut to exterior windscreen shot as Margot opens driver's door. She looks confused.

Margot: Can I get in?
Woman: Please…please do.

Margot gets into driver's seat. For a
beat, they both stare out of the
passenger window; doomed sisters? Then
they turn to one another, perhaps an echo
of Eve and Margot from earlier?

'Get out, Margot. You know this is bad news.'
'Ssshhhh!'

Margot: I'm sorry…but I didn't see your
sweater…in the trunk.
Woman: Sokay…sokay…I think I might have
left it back…at the…motel.
Margot (laughing nervously): Oh…okay.

'Bullshit. Get out you, silly cow.'
'Hey, you're hooked.'

Both women look through the windscreen
again. Margot looks confused. The woman
looks distraught and expectant. Cut to
swaying car-keys in ignition. Margot grabs
the car keys, turns towards the woman and
gasps.

Margot: My god! What's that? What is that
on your neck?

The woman covers the left side of her
neck with her hair. The viewer doesn't
see the mark but presumes that it's the

same as the wound we saw on the right side.
Woman: Yep…I mean, no…no, it's fine. Can you please start the car?
Margot: Sure…I…

As Margot starts the car, the woman opens the passenger door and dives out.

Margot: What the fuck?

The camera opens out to a wider shot. The woman kicks the passenger door shut and rolls away from the car. Inside the car, the seat belt springs to life, whips across Margot's torso and slots home. It holds her tight. Too tight. Pins her to the seat.
Margot is stranded in the car. She is the new terrified woman. She starts to jerk her body but the belt gets tighter.

Margot: Help!…Where the fuck are you going? Help me.

Cut to woman's pathetic figure. She's is on her knees, mumbling, weeping. The car is revving loudly. Cut to car interior. Margot's bare feet are trying to work the pedals, but they are inoperable. She is distraught.
Margot screams loudly as the car screeches off.

Cut to medium shot of the woman on her knees. She is holding her hands over her mouth, rocking back and forth, groaning. The camera zooms in to her face as she whispers:

Woman: I'm… so…sorry…I'm…so… sorry…

Cut to bird's-eye view. The woman limps towards the rocks that Margot just climbed. Conveniently she finds Beacham's Stetson. Places it on her head. She looks back at the road and the rapidly departing car and starts to descend.

Blackout.

During the blackout we hear the loud, powerful car engine. Below this we hear Margot whimpering. Fade to medium close-up, exterior windscreen shot of Margot's face—tear-soaked, sweating, mascara running. Cut to interior of car. It is clear she has no control over the car's controls: brakes, accelerator, gears, steering wheel. Her bare feet pound the pedals in impotent rage. Cut back to Margot's profile through the windscreen where we see the demonic seat belt tighten even more. Margot gasps. Here comes the electrical hum, more erratic than before, sounding like a trapped wasp.

Subtitles:
mnmnvmfnm…pkpeidjin…Hjoehuvfuon…keoillm
ieuuu

We then see movement behind Margot. Cut to back seat of car. The seat belt in back is as demonic as its counterpart in front. It moves, snakelike, starts to wrap itself around Margot's neck. It loops around her throat. Tightens. Pins her head back on to the headrest. Then it slots home with a loud click. Margot starts to choke. Eyes too wide with horror.
A gentle whirring sound—another one—can be detected below the engine and Margot's choking. This is accompanied by two black plastic arms sliding out of either side of the headrest. Two syringes then slide out of these plastic arms. It's an elaborate set-up. Cut to extreme close-up. Margot's eyes are moving from side to side with purest terror (think *Texas Chainsaw Massacre*, dinner scene). She tries to jerk her head forward but this only chokes her more. Camera zooms out slightly so we see empty syringes, turn and head towards the bottom of Margot's neck. Zoom in to extreme close up of Margot's face. We don't see the syringes do their dark work but Margot—again—does a decent job of convincing us. The camera slowly zooms out again (It's a busy scene!) to show the syringes, now

full of Margot's blood, tuck themselves
back into the headrest. Margot is now
coughing, choking, whimpering like a
snared animal. The back seatbelt unclicks
and snaps back into its previous
position. Margot gasps, holds her hands
to her throat, red face, eyes watering,
sweat pouring, choking. Two neat trails
of blood work their way from the neck
wounds down Margot's collar bones and on
to the front of her white dress.

Blackout

'Holy Christ! What are we watching?'

'Strong stuff, no?'

'Shit … I don't know, if I can carry on.'

Lena paused the film.

'So, what's the deal. It's a vampire car that uses blood as fuel. Is that why all the cars are breaking down, cos there's no oil?'

'No idea.'

'Or, it is some kind of violent, patriarchal avenger…it only does this to women, right?'

'Interesting reading.'

'Whatever, it's…it's pretty sick, right? Your girl almost looks like she doesn't know what hit her.'

'What?…well, that's her job. It's called acting.'

'Yeah, I dunno. It looks like she isn't acting. Like the producers, directors or whoever didn't tell her that shit was going to happen in that car.'

'Erm, I don't think it really happened, Lena. Special effects.'

'I know…I dunno, there's something wrong with this film.
I feel it…deep.'
'Well, it's not a classic…I'll give you that.'
'No, I don't mean that…I don't really know what I mean,
but something feels bad here. Doncha feel it?'
'No, I doncha. Since when do you say doncha?'
'Fuck off.'
'Shall we carry on watching?'
Lena pulled a face which was hard to describe.

> During the blackout we hear 'Beacham's
> chopper' ease on to the soundtrack. Fade
> to mid-shot of chopper hovering amongst
> the blue. Cut to close-up of pilotless
> cockpit. Cut to helicopter looking down
> at the Mustang speeding into frame. Shot
> held until car is almost out of sight.
> Cut to Margot's panicking face through
> windscreen. She is trying to look up at
> the helicopter.
>
> Margot: What do I do, Beacham? I need you
> now, old man.

'You bumped him off you retard.'
'We don't know that for sure. And retard?'
'Off the list?'
'Off the list.'

> Margot sweats, breathes heavily. There is
> a bruise across her throat where the seat
> belt held her in place for the 'transfusion'.

The trails of blood on her dress have dried and are so symmetrical that they look like part of the design—gory Laura Ashley.

Cut to car interior and the speedometer at 80 mph. Series of crosscuts—as earlier—between speedometer and Margot's terrified face. Once again, the speedometer eventually hits its max of 140 mph.

Margot is mumbling incoherently (is this perhaps her alien dialect?).
Margot turns her head and we realise that the demonic seatbelt in back has more work to do. She looks down at her feet. The seatbelt wraps itself around her ankles, secures her legs against the seat. Tightly.

Cut to close up of Margot.

Margot (Desperate, helpless and breathless):
No…no more…stop…please!

The whirring sound—as earlier—kicks in. This time, the plastic arms come out from below the driver's seat. The syringes head for the juicy flanks of Margot's bound calves. Extreme close-up of Margot screaming; camera travels from whole face to eyes, one eye and then the other, then mouth, back to whole face. Margot blacks out.

Blackout.

'Shit, this is grim, Ben, grim.'
'It's not a barrel of laughs, you're right.'

Short blackout. Fade to Margot passed out
at the wheel. Perhaps we panic for a
second before we remember she isn't
driving.

Blackout

During this blackout we continue to hear
the car's engine. Fade to Margot slowly
coming back to consciousness. Momentarily,
the camera reflects her blurred vision
(Vaseline on the lens?). She looks around
the car until her gaze settles on car
radio. Margot turns the radio on. Heavy
static sound. Each time she turns the
dial she is horrified anew, hearing the
following:
The electric hum (no subtitles).
Turns dial.

Yes…you…do (Eve's voice repeated on a
loop—we hear this a number of times).
Turns dial.

Heavy coughing, spluttering, choking
(same as behind frosted glass door).
Turns dial.

Animal sounds, raucous male laughter(as above).
Turns dial.

Cunt man. Cunt man. Kill this man…kill this man if he is like this again.
Turns dial.

Beacham's voice fights through static. (Throughout Beacham's monologue, the camera stays on Margot's face. She makes a catalogue of noises and facial expression, accompanied by nodding and shaking of the head).

Beacham: Hey, Margot, Beacham here from beyond…don't ask, just listen. I'm here to help, girl. Okay, now, for you to get out of this sticky mess, you need to be smart and quick, like that last bitch. No, don't answer. I caint hear ya. If you don't get out…well…you can guess what'll happen. I don't wanna be too…descriptive, girl but…this vehicle'll suck you dry. Every hour it'll take a good, long drink outta ya. So, you gotta do like that last bitch, ya know. You gotta pull up when you see a hitcher. Don't worry, you'll see one. And then you gotta convince em to get in this bloodsucker and drive whilst you skedaddle. Stick with the boot ruse like the last…girl. Okay, girl? Cos, when they open the trunk that releases that sunbitchin' seat belt and you slide on over and convince em that they need to drive. Got that? Ya hear me? Don't answer, I know you do, girl. One last thing, it's gotta be a woman. This vehicle is real choosy. Very straight, don't like guys. Good luck, girl. Missing ya. Over and out.

Cut to medium-shot of Ringo's Diner on route 66.

The door swings open under the red neon sign. Eve walks out. She turns and laughs at voices behind her. She puts her heavy-looking rucksack down. Lights a cigarette. Eve checks her watch. Cut to close up of digital watch's big red numbers: 5:07 PM.

Eve: Come on, baby. Where are ya?

Cut to Margot through windscreen. She is now clearly looking out for hitchers. Margot babbles and then is more coherent. Practising her lines.

Margot: Erm, okay, hi…yeah, you're welcome, yeah please get in…can you…could you…would you please mind driving, please?…I…I…need a rest, ya see…yeah, that's right…in the trunk, it's in there, I'm sure…okay, that's right…you slide on in and I'll jump the fuck out (pounding the dashboard). Fuck. Beacham, you better be right…please be right…please be right.

Cut back to Eve frowning. She places hand over her eyes and looks up at the 66. The road is empty.
Cut back to Margot who turns on the radio again. She's full of panic and seems to want more information from Beacham. Instead we hear the sound of a match being struck. Silence. Then two, almost simultaneous, exhalations. Margot weeps as she hears the conversation with Eve, last night in their cold, 'juiceless', candle-lit room. We see it in flashback.
Flashback: Interior. Camera hovers above Eve and Margot as they smoke in blue light.

Eve: You gonna do that thing, at work… tomorrow?
Margot: Thing?
Eve: Yes, the thing. You know what I'm talking about, baby.
Margot: I…I'm scared, Eve.
Eve: Oh, baby…we gotta get outta here. We're dying. Can't ya feel it? We're drying up. Do it tomorrow. I'll meet you outside Ringo's. I'm doing the early shift tomorrow. I finish at five. We'll go to LA. We'll do okay there…in LA. People'll like us. We'll do okay in LA.
Margot: What about our stuff?
Eve: What stuff?

Margot and Eve turn towards one another.

Suddenly, Lena and me are jerked rudely back to reality…the fourth wall comes crashing down.

The film was being pirated at a cinema and the 'pirate' momentarily lost their bearings. The camera jerks upwards violently and we see a quick flash of the cinema's ceiling. Then the camera is steady again, points straight back at the screen and at Margot chewing on her lip.

'Hold on…stop it…go back a sec.'

'What? Why?'

'Just go back.'

I eased the cursor back and forth, following Lena's instructions.

'There, yeah…no forward…no back a bit more…there. Stop. Shit. Look.'

'What?'

'There, dumb arse. There…look… the…oh what do you call…the decorative thing…on the ceiling?'

'What, the cornice?'

'Yeah, cornice. Look at it then.'

'I am. What about it?'

'It's the Ritzy. Look. That is the cornice at the Ritzy…the old Ritzy, by the looks of it.'

'I don't know. Is it?'

I looked more closely. The frozen image was a little blurry.

'How comes you didn't spot this yesterday?'

'I don't know. I just didn't. That's weird.'

'You were probably still recovering from your second wank after that love scene.'

'Funny.'

Lena leapt forward onto her knees. She grabbed the laptop and sort of shoved it in my face.

'Oh, come on…look, you must recognise it. You used to go there regularly, didn't you? Back in the day? I mean, you still do. I mean, maybe the cornice hasn't even changed. They probably gave it a lick of paint. It must be the Ritzy. Fuck. A pirate at the Ritzy way back when. When? Now, that's quite interesting. Now, you've got what they call in the movies, a lead. Considering you can't find fuck all about this thing on the net you can do a bit of actual, real detective work. It'll give you something to do on your fucking sabbatical, Columbo.'

Lena's statement was bang on. I did end up having something to do on my sabbatical. I really did.

'Okay, I guess you're right. It's worth checking. So, do you want to see the finale? What there is of one?'

'Sure, but just one more thing.'

'What?'

'Columbo reference, twat.'

Margot sees sign: Ringo's Diner—2M.

Cut to close up of Margot. Distressed. Chewing her bottom lip.
Cut to Eve. Distressed. Chewing her bottom lip.
Cut to Margot.
Cut to Eve.
Cut to flashback of Margot and Eve smoking in bed.
Cut to Eve.
Cut to Margot.
Cut to bird's-eye view of the car speeding towards Ringo's Diner and towards Eve. It looks—again—as if the car won't stop in time. It screeches and does the 360-degree spin again. Cut to medium shot; car perfectly positioned in front of diner. Eve between car and diner, looking startled. Margo looking startled. As if she did not want to stop. Eve runs towards the car. The car throbs away, a hungry animal waiting to pounce.

Eve: Baby, what the fuck? What—

The car revs, loudly, as if answering Eve.

Margot: Stop...Eve...don't move. Eve, do not touch this fucking car, ya hear me?
Eve: What? How can I get in if I don't touch it?

Eve moves closer. The car revs again.

In the background we see faces pressed against the window of Ringo's Diner.
Eve moves closer. The car responds by revving again. Seemingly hungry for Eve.

Margot: Eve…godammit, I mean it, baby. Do not move another muscle. Trust me…you trust me don't ya? You don't think I'm making it up, do ya?

The car revs. Louder still.

Eve: I don't…what's goin' on, baby. We're going to LA. Remember?

Cut to a big man who looks like a cowboy, coming out of the doors of Ringo's Diner.

Big man: Eve, everything okay?

As Eve turns to look at the big man, the car screeches away. Eve's face collapses. Cut to Eve looking at the back of the car speeding away to LA on the 66.

Blackout

'What the fuck? So, that's it.'
'That's all folks. Either the pirate quits filming—maybe got caught—or that's it, finito.'
Lena looked wistful. Sort of wriggled her nose.

'Shit…poor Margot. Your gal is still out there in the filmic netherworld strapped into the car from hell, having her blood sucked.'

Lena got closer. Took my can of beer and hers and put them on the bedside table. She whipped off her t-shirt and struck a saucy pose.

'Well, hey, not that that thing has put me in the mood, but…'

I was woken by the rain and Lena's snoring. It was about midnight and I had an overwhelming urge to check out the ending of *Driveshaft* again. It couldn't have ended that way, could it? I woke Lena with my fidgeting. Lena went out to make tea while I tried to set the film up. I went on to YouTube but no *Driveshaft*. I tried again and again. No *Driveshaft*. I tried other titles: *Crankshaft; Vampcar, Horrorcar, Deathdrive*, etc but no luck. I tried *Margot Kidder movies*, no luck. I tried *car horror, cult horror, car cult horror*, closest was a thing called *The Car* from 1977, but no *Driveshaft*.

Lena brought back tea and snacks.

'What are you doing?'

'I can't find it.'

'Find what? Your John Thomas? Here, I'll help you.'

'No…seriously. *Driveshaft*. It's not there anymore. I mean, we did see it, right?'

'See what?'

'Very funny.'

'Come on, people take stuff down all the time.'

'Yeah, but…'

'But what?'

'Well, first of all, it apparently didn't exist in the first place, then it pops up—for one night only—and then disappears again.'

Lena looked sceptical.

'Look, to be quite frank, quite frank and earnest, my dear, I don't give a hoot. The thing gave me the creeps anyway. I'm glad it's gone.'

'Lena?'

'What?'

'Do you often get nosebleeds?'

'What the fuck?'

After I cleaned her up, Lena said that she hadn't had a nosebleed for a while, a long while. She was sat at the kitchen table, leaning forward and pinching the bridge of her nose. It was a gusher. Her t-shirt was soaked and mine was pretty gory. It sounds mean but Lena's voice sounded funny as she pinched her nose and explained.

'I hate these fucking things. I had a real spate of these when we—me and mum—went to Dungeness one year. We always went to fucking Dungeness, when I was a little kid. My mum was a photographer. She said it was the weirdest landscape on earth. And had the best light. Yeah, it was weird, nosebleed nearly every fucking day. Like a bloody geyser, I was. I don't remember the reason for them. Just remember having cotton wool up my nose half the fucking holiday. Are you laughing at me?'

I told her no and kissed her nose.

'Weird isn't it, Leen. All those nosebleeds in the film. Maybe, the film brought it on somehow. Well, you said yourself that it was weird…and it is…it is weird. The film, your nosebleed, all this rain.'

'So, how does a film bring on a nosebleed?'

'I don't know.'

I shook my head. Threw another bloody tissue in the bin.

'I don't know what I'm saying. I think I need some sleep.'

Lena sat up.

'Think it's stopped.'

She grabbed my left hand and placed it on my heart.

'Repeat after me. It's only a movie…it's only a movie.'

Lena stood up and took my hand. She led me back to the bedroom.

The next morning, I woke up in bed with a hangover. We hadn't drunk that much so it was odd. It was as if *Driveshaft* had caused it. Scenes from the film rattled around in my head. I had a tiny residue of a car engine revving away in a corner of my mind. I rolled over and mumbled Lena's name, reached for her. No Lena. Just a yellow post-it on the pillow. Lena's scrawl ran across it diagonally:

Gone home to clean up. Phone Ritzy!
X

I smiled at the note and kissed it. I needed to eat.

Annie's Café

Annie's café was a two-minute walk and I almost salivated as I pictured one of her fry ups. They were big and just above bog-standard. It was raining. I opened the squeaky door and saw Annie at the counter, smiling.

'Ah, I'll have to get some WD40 on that fecking door. All right, Benny, how's yer sabbatical? Ah, that's okay, don't bother wiping yer feet.'

'Oh, sorry, Annie. Erm…yep, it's going okay, thanks.'

'Well, I really could do with one of them meself but I couldn't leave that poor fecker back there in the kitchen to fend for himself. Can you imagine?'

Annie was talking about her husband, Declan.

'I can't. I'd fear for him on his own, Annie.'

'Yeah, poor imbecile. Has trouble wiping his own arse. And to think that that George Clooney asked me to drop everything and live with him. Wanted me to settle down in LA.'

My head swam at Annie's next line.

'People'll like you in LA, Annie, he said. I can't leave him, George, I said as I slid out of his four-poster. I just can't leave the poor helpless, shitty-arsed fecker.'

A volley of colourful language from the kitchen made the rain-soaked punters at Annie's roll up with laughter. Annie took my order and I sat down and gazed out at the rain. Annie brought my tea over. Broke my trance.

'Jesus…will it ever feckin' stop?'

'Think the ark is coming, Annie.'

'Well, I wouldn't mind. Could do with shifting those feckin' kittens.'

Annie shuffled off, chuckling. I gazed out the window again. I'd hate to have seen my face. My mind was a jumble of noise and colour: Lena's nosebleed, Margot Kidder and mascara and lipstick; a blue and white car shimmering in desert heat; that pulsing electrical hum; Beacham's blood-soaked shirt; the machine-gun hail and the weird orange light from the corner shop.

'You want to watch that now, Benny. Daydreaming will land you in the shite. Believe me, I know.'

Annie plonked an enormous steaming plate of calories in front of me. She was just about to head back to the kitchen when she wandered to a table by the window, picked something up, wandered back. I looked up as she put the salt cellar down in front of my plate.

'Here are, Benny, you might be needing a pinch or two of this.'

I thought there was something a little extra in Annie's eye as she said this. I wolfed down her fry-up in record time. I thanked her and got another filmic flashback as the café door squeaked open and shut. I headed home with a full stomach. I needed a nap.

I managed a short one, fitful and dream-filled. I am naked walking across the desert when I spot Margot, swaggering my way, 'come-hither-ness' embodied. I feel embarrassed at my nudity and am aroused—this was very much the case when I awoke—and worry that Margot sees this. She does, pauses, adjusts her Stetson, points at my modesty and laughs.

I was woken by a real car engine, revving away outside. I saw Lena's *post-it* still on the pillow, sprang up with surprising energy, looked up the Ritzy number online. Despite Annie's restorative fry-up, I was still a little fuzzy when I phoned the cinema.

'Hello, Ritzy cinema, Ben speaking. How can I help you?'

'Hi Ben, ha-ha, this is Ben.'

'Hi Ben. Ha-ha'.

'Erm…this is going to sound weird, Ben…but do you keep records for the old Ritzy, you know before it was done up?'

'No, sorry mate…Ben. When we refurbed in ninety-six, we got rid of the old records, died with the old cinema.'

'Oh, sugar, that's a shame, Ben.'

'What you after, Ben? I might be able to help; you never know.'

'Ah, it's about a film that was shown there a long time ago.'

'How long? What year?'

'I'm not totally sure that I know, Ben.'

'Yes…you…do.'

'Pardon?'

'I said, that's a shame.'

'Okay…erm…that's…okay, anyway, thanks, Ben.'

'Oh, hold on somethings just popped into my head. 1988, you say?'

'Erm…no, I didn't but…'

'Ah, in that case. I know that the manager during that time was a guy called Frank…in fact he looked after the place forever, did Frank. Bit of a legend, you know. He was an old mate of my dad, Ben senior or Big Ben as we called him. I think he's still alive, Frank that is. If he is, he lives, or used to, just off Brixton Hill. I used to go there as a kid, with my dad, you know. I'll give you his address. Don't have his phone number, doubt if Frank's got a mobile. You got a pen, Ben?'

What the hell was going on? Did I mishear him—Ben—at the Ritzy? Did he really say that line from the film and then tell me I'd said that date? I'm still not sure but I cracked on with my Columbo style detecting, as Lena called it, and consulted a Thomson Local. I'd kept one, out of nostalgia mostly, and soon found Frank's address and land-line number and gave him a ring.

The phone was answered by a cough. It went on for a good thirty seconds. I was about to give up when a broad South London accent answered (think Dennis Waterman).

'Shit, sorry about that … hello?'

'Hello, Frank? I'm so sorry to bother you so early…not that it's that early but…erm…this is going to sound weird but…'

More coughing.

'Sorry, I got your number from the Ritzy cinema in Brixton.'

'Yeah…okay…and?'

Suddenly it dawned on me, a sort of clearance in the fog, that what I wanted to say to Frank, to ask him, sounded like…well…bollocks. I lost my confidence and it showed.

'Erm…well it's about this, Christ, I'm sorry, maybe I shouldn't…erm—'

'No, maybe you shouldn't, mate.' Frank put the phone down.

I put my phone down—literally—on the table.

You, arsehole. I meant me, not Frank. It was a bad start to the *Driveshaft* investigation. I started flipping my phone up into the air and catching it when it rang. It was Frank.

'Frank?'

'Look, why don't you come on over? I have a hunch what this might be about. What's yer name?'

'Ben.'

'Okay. Got a pen, Ben?'

Frank

It flew by. Flew by so quickly. From the visit to Frank's place, which I'm about to share, to the—as it were—finale. It was as if things had been sped up. Like when you zoom forward at 2x on the remote, most unsettling, but at least it meant that the whole thing was over quickly.

By the time I got to Frank's place I was drenched. He only lived about a mile from me so during the hiatus in the rainfall that afternoon I decided to venture outside. After about a minute of leaving my flat, the rain was back and then some. Hailstones as big as, okay not golf balls, but big enough, pounded the streets. There were stories of broken windshields the next morning, but I never believe those—too far-fetched.

Frank lived on the second floor of a handsome council block in Brixton. As I turned the corner and went to make my way up the second-floor stairs, I was blocked by three hefty teens in hoods. I was expecting the worst, but they were polite, moved aside and one even apologised. That was when I got hit by another *Driveshaft* moment. The teens were arguing about money. One of them was belligerent about having paid back what he owed, another was less convinced. Anyway, the argument ended when one of the teens repeated, yes…you…do, over and over, in that annoying, insistent teenage way. I was spooked and my mind—obviously—floated back to Eve in *Driveshaft* encouraging Margot to kill her boss. I tried to shrug it off as coincidence, but it was too late. It was in there and I was rattled.

I knocked on Frank's door. He asked who it was before opening.

'Hi Frank, it's Ben. We spoke earlier. I've come to speak to you about…'

The door opened quickly and there was Frank. A man in his early to mid-seventies, grey hair and beard, sparkling, slightly rheumy, blue eyes and a palpable benevolence. It was weird how much Frank had changed his tune—from cutting the call to redialling and inviting me over, took all of a minute. Frank looked like Beacham from *Driveshaft*. It was a fact that I tried to deny but couldn't. There was no getting away from it. At the start of the evening he looked quite like him, by the end, the resemblance was uncanny. Also, the more he talked, the more he acquired Beacham's Southern State's drawl. Although at the start of the evening he was, like I said, pretty broad south London. Frank shook my hand firmly and invited me in.

'Okay, how you doing, Ben? Nice to meet you. Come in. Take a seat. Let's get this over with… if it's about what I think it is.'

I followed Frank into his flat. He walked slowly and with a slight limp. Frank's place was small but comfortable. It was too hot and had a slightly damp atmosphere. Frank led me into the cosy front room and gestured towards an armchair by the window. Two small lamps, with conical orange shades, lit the room.

'Sorry for my rudeness on the phone, but it so unusual to get a call on the landline, you know…and when you do…it's usually some kind of scam.'

'That's okay…I get it. No problem, Frank.'

'You okay there? Warm enough?'

'Yeah, fine. Cheers.'

'You can keep an eye on the rain from there.'

'Yeah…my god…is it ever going to stop?'

'Erm, hey look Ben, before we start…I was just going to get myself a drink. Can I get you one? Beer? Whisky? I like a whisky, in this weather. Perks me up, you know.'

'Erm, bit early for me but, oh…okay, why not. That'll be great. Small one please, Frank.'

Frank chatted as he fixed the drinks in the kitchen.

'Yeah…they say it's in for another week…the rain. Some of them religious cranks are saying this is it, the end is nigh and all that Armageddon shit, you know. Noah, the second coming. Get em around here all the time—religious cranks that is, not biblical characters.'

Frank laughed at his own joke. So did I. It was good.

'Always bugging me. I must look like a lost soul or something, Ben.'

'Yeah, they don't take a hint.'

'That's for sure.'

Frank returned with the drinks.

'That enough?'

'Wow. Yeah, that's a big one.'

'Well, I get very few visitors, these days, Ben. So, here's to it. Whatever it is.'

'Cheers.'

'Cheers.'

We raised our glasses. I took a sip. The whisky went to work quickly, warming the cockles. Frank exhaled loudly and leaned back in his armchair. I looked out the window and saw the three teens flash across the green below Frank's block. I turned back to Frank. An orange glow, from the lampshade, hovered around him and I thought of the film and the light in the bathroom with Margot. Frank cleared his throat.

'So, who gave you my details, Ben?'

'Ah, a guy called Ben. Works at the Ritzy. Says he knows you; his dad was—'

'Big Ben! Christ! Little Ben is still there. That's great, lovely kid, real chip off the old block. Yep, big Ben was a good friend, God rest his soul. What a beautiful man. Fuck, do I miss him.'

Frank shook his head, laughed.

'Well, Ben, I gotta be honest…I don't really like to talk about this…business too much. You know, it has…well, not sure how to put it…eaten into my life somewhat. I don't want to bore you with too many details but before I start…I just want to warn you to be careful. Look, I don't want to freak you out but…don't know quite how to put it but…erm…'

Frank's voice and demeanour became grave.

'… erm, it'll be good to have a large pinch of salt with you at all times, from now on, you know.'

A tiny tremor made its way up my spine. Salt. A pinch of salt. I had a flashback to Annie's meaningful look when she put the salt cellar in front of me. Frank took a big sip of whisky and sighed long and loud.

'Now, I'll tell you all I know about *Driveshaft*…erm, that is what this is about…isn't it, Benny?'

I nodded as a siren invaded our space for a moment. Its blue light flashed across Frank's small front room. I wondered if the teens had been pinched.

'Erm…yeah, it is. *Driveshaft*, definitely *Driveshaft*.'

Frank took a gulp of whisky and nodded to himself.

'Okay…okay, then. Well…I'll try and tell it straight, you know in the right order, but…I'm getting old and I forget stuff … so, if I wander sometimes, please forgive me.'

'Of course, take your time, Frank.'

'And…well, so much has happened since…that night…the night we showed it at the Ritzy.'

'It's okay, Frank. Please take your time.'

Frank coughed. Put down his whisky and rubbed his legs. Settled back into his armchair.

'Okay, here we go. Ready?'

I nodded.

'So, come with me please, to a wet evening in November 1988. I'd been managing the Ritzy for maybe a couple of years by then. It was the days of bad coffee and good homemade cakes. We were doing okay. Bit random, as you know. But our hearts were in it. We'd do stuff like double bills with the same colour, you know, *Blue Velvet* and *Electra Glide in Blue; The Red Shoes* and *Red River*; horror and sci-fi all-nighters and the like. Random, bit camp and a bit left, and fun—mostly.'

I smiled acknowledgement.

'Yep, I was under-age, but I snuck into those horror all-nighters. Our paths probably crossed once or twice.'

Frank nodded, smiled. He paused and it looked, for a second, as if he didn't want to go on. But, he did.

'Anyway. I remember the first weird thing—and there were many that night—was when the can arrived from the distributor.'

'Film can?'

'Yep. I used to love receiving those. 'specially on Tuesdays…which was the weird film night or The Tuesday Club, as it was actually called. Like getting a Christmas present, it was. Loved taking them up to the projection room…hey, Big Ben was up there sometimes, at the controls, ya know.'

Frank smiled ruefully.

'So, anyway, the can arrives—no digital stuff then, of course. So, I take a hold of it. I had heard nothing about it—*Driveshaft*—nada, not a dickie-bird. And, back then, you know, I had my ear to the ground, as far as film was concerned. I tried to find Robbie. He was in charge of running The Tuesday Club. I tell ya, some of the films that turned up. Shit. Robbie was a connoisseur of the cultish, that's for sure.'

'Can you remember any others?'

'Yeah, some of em.'

Frank looked up to the ceiling and closed his eyes in concentration. He swirled his drink slowly. The ice cubes made a soothing sound.

'Yeah, stuff like *Harold and Maude, Two-Lane Backtop*…and *Repo-man*…funny enough, we showed another one with Margot Kidder…*Black Christmas*. You know it?'

'I certainly do.'

Frank laughed.

'Man, that film was out there…way out there. That swearing, grunting, heavy breathing serial killer…ha-ha. They just wouldn't have the gumption to make a movie like that now; clever film, mind…well-made film.'

'Sure was. Minor classic.'

We took a sip of whisky at the same time. Frank smiled, glint in his eye.

'Can a classic be minor?'

'I…'

'Just kidding. Anyway, I was kinda worried about showing *Driveshaft*. Didn't know a thing about it, you know. Just had this weird feeling…but I wanted to stay with the spirit of the old Ritzy, you know, take a risk. Wish I hadn't. Really wish I hadn't.'

Frank looked down at his glass. Looked up again. His eyes even more rheumy.

'So, anyway, the can comes with no info apart from it's an X certificate and that it's only sixty-odd minutes long—I remember numbers pretty well for some reason. Anyway, I wasn't expecting much of an audience, so I wasn't overly concerned, you know. And you know what? come to think of it…the weather was just like this. Constant rain. That's right…I remember the delivery driver being soaked.'

Frank put down his drink and rubbed his legs again. More vigorously this time.

'Shit.'

'You okay, Frank?'

'Yep…I'm gonna go grab a snack—and some more firewater. Want some?'

'No, I'm okay, thanks. Cheers.'

Frank struggled out of his seat. Made his way to the kitchen.

'Yeah, I can really knock this stuff back some days, you know. Bit of a worry but, hey, it's my only vice…nowadays. Yeah, funny, this really reminds of the winter of eighty-eight, this constant rain, the general feel. Weird'.

Frank shuffled back in with a small glass bowl full of peanuts in one hand, large whisky in the other. He smiled warmly. Now he really began to resemble Beacham; his voice started to take on a North American flavour. As he sat, he started to chuckle. He leaned forward with the bowl of nuts.

'Nut?'

'No…no thanks.'

'Shit, that sex scene…oh man, what kinda career move was that for Margot? Jesus, I freaked…we all freaked. I wanted to shout out, stop the picture, stop the picture but…well…ya know, we were just so…shocked. We just froze. And then there was…Anthony.'

'Anthony?'

'Yeah… Anthony was this homeless guy. We used to let him in, ya know, if the weather was terrible. Give him a break, ya know. Make him some tea. Anyway, Anthony was laughing his head off. He was in fits during the sex scene. Most of the other punters, well, they were shushing Anthony. Christ, the guys in that audience musta been cock-a-hoop—'scuse the phrase. To them it was Christmas come early—'scuse the phrase. Lord…these two beautiful young women—well, I don't need to paint it, you know yourself. You have seen it, right, Ben? *Driveshaft*, I mean.'

'Yeah, I saw it on YouTube…but it's…disappeared into thin air. Like it was never there.'

'Yeah, don't surprise me none…has a life all of its own.'

Frank became deadly serious, for a moment.

'You know that doncha, Ben?'

I nodded earnestly. I too felt deadly serious.

'Yes, Frank, I'm beginning to.'

And in technicolour flashback was Lena's nosebleed and the creepy teens and Annie and LA and her salt and little Ben at the Ritzy and right in front of me was Frank looking and sounding—more and more—like Beacham.

'Anyhow, a couple of us, we went down to shush Anthony. Took him a cuppa tea. I sat with him for a while. Calmed him down. So, that kinda distracted us, ya know. So, well…bottom line we didn't stop the film.'

Frank took a big gulp of whisky and exhaled a long, loud sigh through his nose.

'You know all the nosebleeds…in *Driveshaft*?'

I leaned forward. Lena's bloody nose flashed across my mind again.

'Yeah…I do.'

'Well…we had seventeen punters in that night—told ya I was good with numbers—and twelve of em had had a nosebleed by the time the lights came up. That's when the weirdness began. Shit, you couldn't make it up. You don't think that, do ya?'

'Think what, sorry?'

'That I'm, making it up?'

'No…no, not at all. Why would I think that?'

'Well, I've told a few folk…this…tale over the years, ya know…and some give me that look…like…sure, buddy, sure. Especially, when I have a whisky inside me, ya know—and, I tend to take more of this stuff than I used to. They think I'm just a drunk ole geezer spouting so much bullshit, ya know.'

'Well, Frank, I believe every last word.'

'You okay, Ben? You look distracted.'

'No, I'm okay…well, I may as well tell you whilst we're on the subject. My girlfriend, Lena, had a nosebleed yesterday, just after we finished watching it…*Driveshaft.*'

Frank stroked his beard and half smiled.

'Innaresting. Does she get em regularly?'

'No. Not since she was a kid.'

'Innaresting.'

Frank looked down at his empty glass while I looked at Frank. I cleared my throat and he looked up.

'So, how about the nosebleeds? At the cinema?'

'Yeah, the nosebleeds. Ya know if it happened now, I reckon it'd be massive, huge. I mean, first off, people would take photos of each other…of themselves and post em here, there and everywhere. Can you imagine? Bloodbath at South London cinema. It'd go viral, as they say.'

'Yep, I think you're right.'

That's when I so very nearly called Frank, Beacham. It took some effort not to do so. I was starting to feel unnerved. Frank continued.

'Anyway, if I remember right—and I probly don't—the first nosebleed occurred just after the fat guy got one…you know, Margot's boss…when he is looking up at the ceiling in his chair, in his office, in the film, ya know. Remember?'

'Yep, I remember.'

'I think it was a couple. They just bombed down the aisle. I don't know if both of em had a nosebleed but the guy definitely did. He was holding it—his nose. They didn't come back, so must have been bad, I guess. Then…I dunno…I think some people just had like a small leakage that maybe they thought was just…well…manageable. Coz only one other guy left during the film—and that was Anthony. He was so restless, bless him. Anyway, it was all kinda subdued, no hysteria…nobody rushing out and screaming. In fact, it was weird…low-key, ya know. Like they didn't want to admit it.'

'How did you know there were twelve of them?'

'What?'

'Nosebleeds. You said there were twelve nosebleeds.'

'Ya know, I don't really know. I just recall…the number twelve. Shit, maybe I'm wrong. Anyway, there were plenty folk looking sheepish, holding tissues to their faces when the lights came up. The toilets were busy for ages afterwards.'

Frank put down his whisky, held his head in both hands and leaned forward.

'You okay, Frank? You don't have to carry on, I…I can go and maybe come back another day.'

'No, no…sokay. I'll try and remember. Stay, please…sokay, Benny. You okay me calling ya Benny, Benny?'

Frank looked up and grinned. I couldn't help but laugh. 'Sure.'

'Hey, Benny, I need to go powder my nose—shit, that's not so funny…considering. Anyway, pardon me…for a minute or so.'

'Sure.'

Frank was halfway out of his armchair when I sort of exploded into life. The sudden movement persuaded Frank back into his seat.

'Shit, sorry, Frank, I almost forgot. Did you notice anybody recording the film?…I mean, the copy I saw on YouTube was pirated from the Ritzy.'

Frank paused, narrowed his eyes and gave me a fairly lengthy stare. He sat back down.

'Ah…okay, you don't look like a Fed, ha-ha…so…well, we had a little arrangement you see, back in the day. Robbie—he was the guy who organised The Tuesday Club—he had friends, ya see, friends who would film the films, the pirates, ya know.'

'Do you know who it was…who filmed *Driveshaft*?'

'No…no, it wasn't always the same dude. I do remember somebody came in late…stumbled up the aisle. Maybe that was the pirate.'

'Do you think they…the pirate, got a nosebleed?'

'I dunno. Why?'

'Because the copy I saw cuts off the beginning and the end, and now I'm guessing that the pirate had a nosebleed and vacated the premises.'

Frank nodded and grimaced, looked down at his feet.

'You okay, Frank?'

'Yeah, yeah…go on, Benny.'

'The pirate guy…or girl…was also jogged or distracted by something about forty minutes in. That's why I'm here. My girlfriend recognized the cornice. Any idea what that might have been? The distraction?'

'No, I… can't help ya there…somebody close by jogged him? Or else, somebody went to the toilet in front of him or got a nosebleed. I dunno, Benny.'

'Yeah, sorry, not sure if it's that important, now.'

Frank started to rub his legs again.

'Shit! Scuse me, Benny, but I really gotta…go, ya know. Don't go anywhere.'

'Sure, Frank. Take your time.'

I looked down at the eyeful of golden liquid at the bottom of my glass. I threw it back and drained the remnants. I put the glass down on the arm of the armchair and looked around Frank's small front room. Frank had a nice collection of books and films and books about films. My head was light and my insides warm from the whisky. I stood up and walked towards a book that seemed to wink at me in the dim orange light of the room. It started to look extremely familiar. I slid the book out and acknowledged it with a grunt and a wry grin. I wasn't surprised that Frank had a copy of *Easy Riders, Raging Bulls* but it's presence just added to the general weirdness. I opened it and saw a message on the inside cover:

Hey Franklin,
Here's to a happy ending, bud.
Too much love.
Big Ben (Xmas 98) x

I tried to smile at the warmth of the message but I got another tingle up my spine. I just felt weird again. More coincidence. Too many Bens and too many Margots. The book suddenly felt cold. I was about to replace it when I heard my name being called. I dropped it beside the armchair and looked out the window, expecting the worst: one of those freaky teens knew my name and was calling me, outside in the rain.

Then I realised it was Frank, sounding distressed. I dashed out into the hallway. Frank was knocking on the toilet door from the inside.

'Benny, in here… fuck, help…quick…here.'

The toilet door opened inwards.'

'Help me. I'm…fuckin' stuck.'

Frank was on the toilet with his trousers around his ankles. He looked to be in some discomfort.

'Ah, maaan. I'm sorry but I just…just can't stand up. Fuckin' pins and needles cripplin' me. Help me up would ya?'

I lifted Frank up from the toilet. I'll spare you the details of what happened next. It's not hard to imagine. Poor Frank. When we eventually returned to the front room Frank kept apologising.

'So, sorry, Benny. It's my dirty little secret. I've kept it to myself…out of superstition mostly, I guess. Ever since *Driveshaft*, I get these bouts of pins and needles—ya know, like Beacham in the car? Man, they almost finish me at times. I thought I had MS but the hospital has given me the all clear…twice. Shit, I just never know when they're gonna hit. But when they do…'

'Sorry to hear that, Frank. Sounds bloody awful. Does other…stuff happen? you know…*Driveshaft*…stuff?'

Frank seemed to stare through me. The pause was uncomfortably long. Then he reeled off this dreadful list.

'Fuck, yeah. How long ya got? Let's see…nosebleeds, seeing members of the cast all over south London, random folk intoning lines from the movie, ubiquitous orange lights, my car playing up somethin' terrible, overexuberant seat belts—shit!…that was the worst so far, that belt got so fuckin' tight across my chest. Felt like a heart attack. Also, I have to deal with this fuckin' irritating deep southern drawl that slowly creeps up on me like a bad cold.'

I had to laugh and was relieved that Frank was aware of it.

'Yeah, I know, I look like the fucker to, doaneye? Beacham, I mean.'

I laughed again and nodded.

'So, yeah, other stuff, for sure, Benny. Ya see, that's why I put the phone down at first, ya know, when you called…coz I was afraid that shit would intensify, come back strong, ya know. But at the same time, I wanted to, I dunno…confront it, I guess. It's funny…when you rang on the landline, I got this tingling in my legs which is always a signal that somethin' is…I dunno…awakenin' or re-awakenin', ya know.'

'I think I do, Frank…I think I do know…now. I hope it's not my fault. Maybe I shouldn't have bothered…ringing you. Shit…I feel so bad.'

Frank leaned forward, looking like a concerned uncle.

'No man, ain't your fault, Benny. It's always been hovering around since that night in eighty-eight. It's been a feature of my life. Sometimes it's funny, sometimes freaky, but it's always there. I guess it's part of my DNA now, ya know.'

He sat back further in his seat and was, again, suffused in the orange glow of his lamp.

'So, Benny, what we gonna do?'

'What do ya…you…mean, Frank?'

Frank pointed at me. He was holding his whisky and half smiling. All orangey and a little sinister.

'Well, you're a part of it now…you feel it doncha? The ball has started to roll, or the dice.'

'I know…I mean, I…don't know, Frank. I'm still sort of coming to terms with things. It's all new to me and weird…plain fucking weird. Feels like I'm stuck in a dream.'

I leaned forward and put my head in my hands. A vision of Lena strapped into the *Driveshaft* car flashed before me.

'You okay, Benny?'

I looked up and there, more or less, sat Beacham. I was staggered but tried not to show it.

'Benny, you okay, bud?'

I had an enormous urge to get out of Frank/Beacham's flat. I'd been drawn into something way beyond me.

'Benny?'

'Yeah…sorry…think so, Frank. I'm just worried about Lena. I'm worried about her after that nosebleed and after the things you've told me and—'

'Hey, hey, Benny, take it easy, I understand. You skedaddle, if ya feel ya need to.'

'I'm sorry to leave you, Beach…Frank. I'll be in touch.'

'Yep…I know you will. And remember, Ben…pinch a salt.'

I shook Frank's hand, told him not to get up. I closed his door quietly and was greeted by rain, the dark, and a giant, cartoon moon. I descended the stairs two by two. The lights in the block all seemed to blink and I jumped at my giant, disfigured shadow. I was convinced that I'd meet somebody from the film grinning malevolently or I'd get a nosebleed or pins and needles, but the only oddness was the enormous, full moon that seemed to watch me. I tried Lena on her mobile but no response. A grotesque image plagued me: Lena haemorrhaging through her nose. Her flat awash with blood (think *The Shining*), crawling on her hands and knees, dying and cursing me; fuck-face this, fuck-face that. I ran the rest of the way.

Weirdo Academics

When I got home it wasn't as late as I thought. I sat at the kitchen table and looked out at the moon. It was sinister now; mocking me with impassive 'mooniness'. Christ! I needed rest; rest and something or somebody to wake me up from the dreamworld I'd been woven, drawn, sewn into. I tried Lena again but no good. I went to bed again. Sleep was elusive. My mind was in a washing machine. Images kept tumbling under and over one another; the film, the visit to Frank's, the moon. They all got jumbled up until I almost believed that the visit to Frank's was a scene from the movie. I got out of bed and wandered into the cold front room. There was that fucking moon again; streaming through the curtains, lighting up my laptop.

Okay, I get it…I get it, moon. There must be something out there, in here, something in here, in this box of digital magic, I thought. So, how about those bleeders who saw *Driveshaft* that night, had fallen victim to its power—through their noses— literally? Surely one of those seventeen punters at the Ritzy with Frank, back in November eighty-eight, had posted something, somewhere, surely. I fed ludicrous lines into the inter-web— again; words and phrases that might dredge *Driveshaft* up from its mysterious, murky depths: *nosebloodfest, nosebleeds at cinemas; Ritzy cult-night horror, public nose-bleeds; cult-this, cult-that, drive-this, drive-that, shaft-this, shaft-tha*t. I went deep into the heart of the web, but no joy. I'd done this before I reminded myself. What's the fucking point? I was starting to flag and droop when I pulled out my joker. How about weirdo academics? Horror movies seemed to attract them. Boom, a new lifeline. I happened across some horror dissertations on a University website, there were some wacky titles, one that I thought might bear fruit; *Blood for Sale: The Neo Vampire Movie* as *Critique of Mass Consumerism*, but no *Driveshaft*. Then I spotted: *Patriarchy on the Rack: 1970s Cult Horror and the Rise of the 'Second Wave'* by Katherine Blake. And there waiting patiently on page thirteen, was a chunky extract about *Driveshaft*. I'd actually tracked something down. It felt great. I pumped a fist and whooped.

The rise of the second wave of feminism, then, seemed to be pushing representations of patriarchy to commit ever more heinous acts against women. This was even—or maybe especially the case—in maverick or outlier horror productions of the 70s, such as Driveshaft, where patriarchy is at its most sinister, sadistic and vengeful.*

Oppressive masculinity comes in the shape of a vampiric car. Margot Kidder, to an extent, reprises Janet Leigh's role as Marion Crane from Psycho. Kidder's character, Margot!,—I am leaving her status as an alien out of the analysis—takes a step further than Leigh's Crane; instead of merely stealing from her chauvinistic employer Margot kills hers. During her escape another male character—this time a benevolent one—goes and dies on her so she is forced to hitch a lift; traditionally a recipe for disaster in the horror film. The driver who picks her up is a distraught woman who jumps out of the car when Margot enters. Margot is then pinned into her seat by a demonic seatbelt. Later in the journey syringes pop out of the headrest and footrest. The syringes—as they did to the original driver— take blood from Margot's neck and legs. We also find out that the car is 'straight' and only accepts female passengers. So women are being sucked dry by the roving vampire car—an attractive light blue Mustang with a white roof.

The car seems an apt metaphor here. During the 1970s the import of ostentatious European sports cars, such as Ferraris, Lamborghinis and Lotuses was on the rise, as were 'souped up' versions of classic American favourites like Mustangs and Thunderbirds. The car was also seen not only as a status symbol for men but was often equated with masculinity and/or sexual prowess. After all, fewer women drove during the 1970s and there were numerous stock jokes about their apparent dubious ability behind the wheel. In fact, during this period, one was more likely to see an image of a woman draped over a car in a bikini rather than driving one.

The penetration by the syringes has obvious connotations to the act of rape. Yet, the extraction of blood takes us into 'neo' vampire territory—George. A. Romero's Martin is a good example of this genre—where contemporary social issues are arguably more prevalent than in more 'traditional' blood-sucker flicks, like the Hammer series. In Driveshaft the women who get into the car literally have the lifeblood sucked out of them. In Margot's case we see a female who has transgressed—not only has she killed her boss but she also has the temerity to be a lesbian

The lesbian love scene in Driveshaft is, to say the least, unusual for an X-certificated horror movie. It is arguably pornography. I could not track down any reviews or articles on Driveshaft, but I would presume that many feminists would view the love scene as gratuitous and designed to titillate a male audience. But I think it is used to highlight that Margot and Eve are on the margins of patriarchal, conservative society and therefore need to be punished doubly: for the murder of a powerful male, as well as, for their sexuality—not only can this bitch drive but she kills men and loves women. She really has to go. She is an outlaw and an outlier who cannot be allowed to escape the clutches of convention; as the ultimate 'other' she must be eradicated by patriarchy.*

**Could also see the scene as a powerful sideswipe at conservative/patriarchal forces within mainstream filmmaking of the time… (but no information available on writer or director).*

**Name of director unknown*

I wondered if Katherine Blake had seen the same version of *Driveshaft* as me and Lena.

Finding Katherine

My next step was to try and find Katherine Blake. She wrote the dissertation almost thirty years ago so I wasn't optimistic. Katherine, though, was easy to track down as she taught at the same university where she submitted her thesis. I sent her a brief e-mail, expressing interest in her work, and attached my mobile number. At the time, I couldn't believe how quickly Katherine responded—as long as it takes to make a cup of tea.

'Hello!'
'Hello, is that Ben?'
'Hi…Katherine? Wow…thanks for getting back so quickly.'
Low electrical hum.
'My god, what's that noise?'
'Erm…I think…hello?'
Low electric hum.
'God, that noise. It's…'
'…you mean you actually read my awful dissertation?'
'No…yes, it was great…I…'
'Ha ha…that's very kind, but…no, it really was not. Anyway—'
Line goes dead. I ring Katherine.
'Hi Katherine, sorry…not sure what's happening with the connection.'
'It's okay…go ahead.'
'Well, you wrote, near the end of your dissertation about a film called *Driveshaft*.'
Low electric hum.

Katherine laughs. 'Yeah…hello…I can't hear you…Ben, are you still there?'

'Hello…ah, that was weird. That noise, it's—'

'Hello…yes…it happens…I—'

Low electric hum.

'Hello?'

'Yeah, Katherine…I'm still here.'

'Yes…I can just about hear you…oh, look, let's meet. We really should.'

'Okay, where?'

'Goodge Street tube? I work close by. Are you free tomorrow?'

'Yes.'

Low electric hum.

'Katherine?'

'Tomorrow…I mean, later today…one pm.'

'One pm?'

'One pm.'

'Okay.'

Line goes dead.

For some reason—probably because I'm extremely judgemental—I'd expected a cerebral looking person, intensely serious, shy perhaps, with glasses and a slight stoop, but Katherine Blake was a tall, handsome woman in early middle age with an impressive posture. Her brown hair was cut short and her eyes were grey and alive with humour. It was strange. Plenty of people milled about around the station but we made a beeline for one another, like magnets, shook hands at Goodge Street station exit and headed into the small coffee bar next door. I followed Katherine through the squeaking glass door.

'Did you hear that?'

Katherine smiled sagely—she did this a lot.

'Yes, I did. Do it again, Ben'.

I did. I opened the door again. No squeak.

I frowned. Katherine smiled.

Two young women were stocking trays with deli goodies and placing them in cold storage under the glass display. They seemed to giggle at me—not us—as we sat down. I was already paranoid after the *Driveshaft* incidents and this didn't help. We ordered coffee. As we settled into our seats it started to rain.

'My god, it just won't give in.'

'Yep, Noah's on the way.'

'Wow, that's weird.'

'What's weird?'

'Oh…just keep hearing that line…the one about Noah and his Ark.'

Katherine smiled rather knowingly.

'Yes? You hearing other stuff too, Ben?

'Yeah…I'm encountering an awful lot of squeaky doors amongst other things.'

She smiled again. Sounds corny and, perhaps predictable, but I felt I'd known Katherine for ages. She put her hand out for me to shake.

'Guess, I should welcome you to the club then, Ben.'

'Okay, which one's that then?'

Katherine laughed as I shook her hand.

'The *Driveshaft* club, of course. It's pretty exclusive.'

'Weird is the word I'd use.'

Katherine repeated the word back at me in a sort of enigmatic way. Her voice was soft and there was a slight twang in the mix. Perhaps American.

'Well, weird, is your watchword from now on, Ben. If you're not used to weirdness…you soon will be.'

Katherine kept her eyes on me as she sipped her coffee. It was quite sexy.

'Talk to me then, Ben.'

'I don't really know where to begin, Katherine.'

'How about with a pastry? This coffee's too wet.'

'Okay.'

I got up and ordered croissants. The waitresses smiled strangely at me again. I sat back down, frowning, as Katherine was putting her mobile phone back in her bag. She looked up, smiled quickly.

'You okay, Ben?'

'Yeah…no…well, I don't really know.'

'Do you…want to start?' Katherine laughed again. 'Sorry, it's just that I sound like a shrink.'

'Well, I think I could do with one right now.'

One of the smiley waitresses brought the croissants over. We thanked her.

'Anyway, our phone call yesterday…that noise. Sounded just like the *Driveshaft* noise. You know, the low humming that is Margot's interior monologue.'

'I do, Ben. I know the humming noise very well …and, yes, I agree, the sound on the phone was just like it.'

Katherine was smiling but it didn't seem to be at me, this time.

'You okay? What's funny?'

'Oh, nothing, it's just—'

Katherine was staring intently over my left shoulder as we spoke. The small smile that she'd been holding for a while slowly began to widen.

'Katherine? You look…distracted.'

'Oh yes, I am. Very much so, Ben.'

I leaned in closer to her.

'Would you care to…share?'

'Of course.'

She leaned in close. I thought for a second that she was going to kiss me. All the time she kept a keen eye on the area behind me, where the young women were. I was about to look around when she grabbed and squeezed my arm.

'Hold it, Ben. Not yet. I think you need to take a few deep breaths first. You may not be ready.'

Katherine had become—like Frank had, at times—grave in her manner. She placed her left hand on top of my right hand.

'Deep breaths? Ready?'

'What? W…why? What's going on?'

'Okay…listen to me. I want you to count to ten, turn around, slowly, and take a look at the waitress—not the one who served us—the other one. But make sure you breathe deeply. Okay?'

'Erm…you're sort of scaring me and I'm not sure I want to look, but…okay.'

I managed to reach seven and began to turn around as slowly and subtly as I could. I rarely gasp out loud but I did when I saw her. I also jerked involuntarily, kicked the table and spilt our coffee. The waitress was young, beautiful, with large hazel eyes, a beguiling and crooked smile and was the spitting image of a twenty-something Margot Kidder.

'Shit. What the fuck!'

I was too loud and the other customers gave me the stink eye. I held up a hand in apology and swung back around to a smiling Katherine.

'You're finding this funny?'

'Don't worry. It happens all the time.'

'What…what do you mean it happens all the time?'

'Well…'

Katherine began her explanation whilst I was half turned and half listening, staring at the impossible waitress. I re-established eye-contact with Katherine when she cleared her throat loudly and 'Margot' disappeared out back somewhere.

'So, as I was saying when you weren't listening…I don't know how to explain the…occurrences. I guess they're beyond explanation. I'm used to them now and…I know this sounds perverse, but I sort of well… accept the twisted games it— *Driveshaft*—plays and try to enjoy them. That electrical hum on the phone yesterday is a typical, and less inventive, example.'

'So, I'm guessing, that…that…there…behind the counter is what you would call a much more inventive example?'

'Yes. Definitely.'

'And is…is it new to you, I mean, somebody transforming into somebody else?'

'No, it's not new to me, Ben. But…it's a good one, nonetheless…a good likeness, don't you think?'

I turned around but 'Margot' was still absent. I leaned in and whispered, incredulous.

'Good! a good one. I'm having fucking kittens…and you tell me it's a good one.'

Katherine smiled, more warmly this time.

'Ben, I know it's a tough ask but try to calm down. You'll learn to take the whole thing with a pinch of salt … eventually.'

I jerked up and almost out of my seat.

'Oh no. Shit…stop! pinch a salt, pinch a bloody salt. That's what Frank said last night. Exactly that. And Angela, yesterday or the day before or whenever. Fuck.'

Again, I said it too loudly. Again, the punters turned and looked at me, as did the waitress who wasn't 'Margot'.

Katherine exhaled a hint of a laugh through her nostrils. She looked so composed like she knew exactly what was going on.

'Frank? Angela?'

'Yeah, he…Frank, used to manage the Ritzy cinema where they showed the film in 1988.'

'Interesting.'

Katherine gestured towards the counter with her eyes. 'Why don't you go and ask for some tap water?' She paused, took a sip of coffee, fixed her eyes on me, again. I was starting to think there was something slightly impish about her. 'Or, another coffee, perhaps?'

I looked towards the counter. I couldn't see 'Margot', but I was curious.

'You know, the thing is, Katherine…well…I have this real thing about Margot Kidder…and I would have loved to have met her when she looked just like that…but she—*that*—isn't her behind there, is it?'

The other waitress eyed me warily as she reorganised the trays under the glass display.

'Go ahead. Go and ask her friend where she is.'

I gave Katherine a rueful look, stood, frowned, sat, stood again and walked to the counter. The young woman extricated herself from the glass display and straightened up, red-faced. Her east European accent was strong.

'Hello, sir. I can help you?'

'Yeah…sorry, but would you mind if I had a quick word with your colleague, the other…young lady?'

'Erm…is everything okay, sir? I can help? Was the coffee not okay? The croissants?'

'No, everything was great…she…it's just, erm…she sort of really looks like a friend's…erm…daughter…I was wondering if it was her.'

The waitress frowned. 'Oh, okay.' She half-turned and called to her friend. 'Lisa…Lisa, some…guy wants to talk you. He thinks he's your daughter's friend.'

The girl shouted from the back. 'What?'

I held my breath, feeling like a nervy, adolescent autograph hunter.

And there she was, suddenly before me; Lisa the waitress, with a very round, pock-marked, face, framed by a blondish bob, smiling and looking absolutely nothing like a young Margot Kidder. I stammered away and said that I was so sorry and that it was the other girl, I meant. Lisa was unimpressed.

'What other girl, mate? It's just me and Magda working today. You all right?'

'No, there was a darker, slimmer, sorry, prettier, sorry, erm…'

Katherine rescued me—or them. She led me away from the frowns of the two young women, ordered more coffee. We sat. Me startled, her amused.

'Shit, where did she go? Where's Margot?'

'Where indeed?'

I excused myself and went to the toilet.

I was thankful that it was my face I saw in the mirror and that there was no orange glow. 'What the fuck is happening?' I said out loud. I jumped at my involuntary verbal spasm, checked under the one cubicle door for a punter. No footwear. I splashed my face and wiped it dry with a paper towel. I held out my arms. 'Come on then. Where are you?'

My voice echoed eerily. I left the bathroom in a hurry.

There was more coffee on the table when I got back. Although, I wasn't sure if coffee was a good idea. A stiff drink seemed more appropriate—one of Frank's generous whiskies. Katherine was putting her phone back in her bag again as I sat. I drank my coffee and watched my hands shake. Katherine looked around the coffeehouse impassively, as if she was recording everything she saw.

'So, Ben, what else has happened to you?'

As I tried to order my thoughts and find a place to begin, Katherine stirred three sugars slowly into her coffee, then sucked the end of her spoon. I cleared my throat.

'Well…first off, Lena—that's my girlfriend, mostly—had a nosebleed after we watched it.'

'Ah, yes, I went through that phase—didn't last long but was pretty messy. I splatted many a draft of my bloody awful thesis with *Driveshaft*-inspired blood and sputum.'

'Nice. Erm, well, then like I said I met Frank last night, you know the ex-manager of the Ritzy…and…well…first these three lads on the stairs, hanging around, you know, teen loitering, menacing but not really menacing, one of them said that line that Eve says in the film—'

'Yes…you…do?'

'That's the one.'

'Yes, that's been the commonest…occurrence, for me, over the years. It can drive you crazy if you're looking or, rather, listening out for it. You know, because people do actually say it.

I suppose it's that pause between the words that confirms it as…official, if you know what I mean.'

Katherine eyed me kindly, almost patronisingly, as she took a sip of her sweet coffee. The light in her grey eyes reminded me of the moon that hung so big and luminous and mocking the night before.

'Anything else?'

'Well, there was the guy, Ben, at the Ritzy. He seemed, I don't know, what's the best word? erm—'

'Programmed?'

'Fuck me. Programmed, yeah that fits. Then Angela—'

'Angela?'

'Yeah, another squeaky door and she said that line that Eve says about LA. And then the pinch a salt echo and—'

'And?'

'Erm…well, Frank of course…he sort of started to look and sound more and more like…'

'Beacham?'

'Erm…yeah. Although he does actually look a little like him anyway…I think.'

'Have you seen Frank in the cold light of day?'

'No. So, you think he might not look like Beacham…at all?'

'I don't know. I'm sure that he could do. I've bumped into a few Beachams over the years, some did actually resemble the guy from the film, after all he has a bit of a generic look. There were others though, who looked nothing like him but transformed into him or his doppelganger, just like Margot, sorry Lisa, over there. It can really get to you at times, like, for example, when your father pops into the kitchen as your father and then pops out again as a bearded American wearing a Stetson and carrying a large, steaming leg of lamb.'

'No way!…fuck…what did you do?'

'What would you do? I went ashen and screamed or the other way around. Anyway, I ran and locked myself in the bathroom. My mum rushed up the stairs. I let her in. Of course, I couldn't tell her. I just said that the dissertation had taken it out of me and that I was worried about passing and then starting on the career ladder, blah blah. I even invented a roguish boyfriend who I said was being, well…roguish.'

'Poor guy. So, what happened in the end, with your dad and Beacham?'

'I went warily back downstairs, holding on to my mum, eyes half closed. I entered the dining room expecting the worst but, lo and behold, my dad was my dad again. Same as Lisa is Lisa again.'

I darted a look towards Lisa, who was still Lisa.

'How long does it last then? This transformation…projection thing?'

'Depends, so far—touch wood—not that long…few minutes, sometimes less. Look, you get used to this stuff. It's been happening to me for years. It's funny now, the whole scene with my dad, it's bloody funny. Most of the…occurrences end up being that way, just—'

'Funny.'

'Exactly.'

'Yeah, well…I guess I'm not at that stage just yet.'

'Anything else?'

'Pardon?'

'I mean, re *Driveshaft*.'

'Oh…well, at the end of the night he…Frank went to the toilet and was gone for ages. Then he shouted for me, and—poor guy—he was stuck on the toilet with—'

'Pins and needles?'

'I usually get pissed off when people finish my sentences, but in your case I'm relieved. Looks like I can't really tell you anything you don't already know. So, what in the name of fuck is going on, Katherine?'

'Good question, Ben. What do you think?'

I exhaled loudly through blubbering lips. Tried to stop my hands from shaking.

'God…who knows? I mean…I haven't really had time to sit and think, been too wound up. Erm, how about a bug or virus…does the film transmit some kind of virus to the viewer?'

'Nice idea. That's a theory I've sort of toyed with over the years. Some kind of virus that infects the viewer and scrambles their fantasy/reality receptors. Or, how about a trip? The film is a drug taken by the viewer which affects a part of their mind and starts to play tricks? Like a drug. A powerful hallucinogen.'

'Yeah, I do, have… felt sort of high.'

'What I've had to learn to do, or try to do, is to, well, not take it too seriously. You know, let it take you, or maybe drive is a better word, where it wants, rather than fighting, resisting it.'

'Resistance is useless?'

'Yes…basically.'

'Like Frank and Angela said…have a pinch of salt to hand. You see, if it is like a trip, one that you have on a hallucinogen that you're not particularly enjoying, then you just have to try and relax and see it through, find a neutral space—isn't that what they say?'

'Who?'

'The drug fraternity…you know, when you are having a bad one. Find a neutral space.'

'I think I've heard it…or something like it. Yeah.'

Katherine took a mouthful of coffee. She flicked her eyes back towards the counter and smiled. My head throbbed and was jammed with questions.

'So, the Frank and Angela salt thing; coincidence?'

'Who knows? Personally, I doubt it. I'd say it's the film— or the virus or the trip doing its stuff. Working on you.'

'But, hold on, Angela's never seen *Driveshaft*, no way.'

'And you think Lisa has or my dad or the dozens of Margots and Eves and Beachams I've bumped into over the years?'

'Shit, sorry…of course. Not thinking straight.'

'How can you at the moment, Ben? You've only just been…indoctrinated.'

I looked nervously up at the counter. The weird thing was that I wanted Lisa to be Margot again. I had this flash fantasy of us hand in hand on a beach in California.

'It's okay, Lisa's still Lisa…for the time being. So, ever had a bad trip, Ben?'

'Yeah, a couple.'

'And?'

'Fucking horrific.'

'Exactly. So that's why you have to try to accept all the things that the film throws up—pardon the phrase—and grin your way through it. Accept it. Accept that for whatever reason, it is toying with you and will probably do so for…well…who knows how long.'

'Great, so… what? why? I mean…how? who?'

'My god…so now you want its *raison d'être*. I have no idea. Whatever you file it under: chemistry, metaphysics, psychology…the supernatural, none of the above are my speciality. Call it what you want but you can't deny it's there. Like I say, accept it and it gets easier. Believe me. You do believe me, don't you? You don't think that, do you?'

'Think what, sorry?'

'That I'm making it up?'

I covered my eyes with one hand, thrust the other one out to indicate the universal stop sign.

'Ben, what's wrong?'

'I'm sorry.'

I leaned in closer to Katherine.

'That's exactly what Frank said, the other night. That line…those lines are straight from the film, aren't they?'

She laughed but it was tighter this time as if she were exasperated but was trying to hide it.

'Yes, I know. Margot says it to Beacham at some point or is it the other way around. Anyway, doesn't matter. I mean, it does matter…you know, to your—our—psychological well-being. *Driveshaft* is a real joker…a real trickster. You see. I couldn't help myself. The line just upped and fell on out of my mouth. I had no control. No volition. It's like that sometimes.'

She picked up her coffee cup with both hands and took a big sip before she continued.

'Look, I know it's freaky, but you already know that something is working away at you, playing with your mind, your perception, has been ever since you saw the film; I mean before Lena's nosebleed and Frank last night and Margot over there today. You know that, right?'

I nodded.

'So, what was the first thing? The first manifestation of the film in the real world?'

As Katherine said it an image from the night me and Lena watched the film flashed before my eyes.

'Fuck, that orange light. There isn't an orange light in the local shop, never has been.'

'Orange light? Like in the bathroom with Margot?'

'Yeah, we peeked through the curtains and out at the rain and I saw an orange light in the local corner shop. Never seen it before, not sure why it didn't strike me at the time. Then, of course, there was Lena's nosebleed. A real gusher'.

She turned up her nose.

'Nasty.'

'And you… how did it first get you, Katherine?'

'For me it was this girl in the library where I was studying. Doing my bloody awful thesis.'

'Katherine, what I read wasn't that bad.'

'Thanks, you really are a bad liar.'

'Anyway, what did she do? Offer you a lift in her blue and white Mustang?'

She laughed. 'That's it, Ben, need a pinch of humour as well as salt. No, there were no Mustangs. She sneezed.'

'Sneezed?'

'Sneezed; and after every sneeze she said, *what the fuck*, instead of excuse me or the equivalent. You know, that's probably the most common phrase in the film.'

'What the fuck?'

'Yes.'

'Okay… then what…a nosebleed?'

'Well, you'd think so…seems logical, right?'

'Right.'

'But no, this thing, this bug or infection or trip, whatever you want to call it is sometimes predictable, even logical, sometimes not.'

'So, what happened?'

'Well, it was—how best to put it?—extremely discomforting. I think that I was so unnerved because it was my first time, I was a *Driveshaft* virgin. Also, I was just so tense and oversensitive at the time, you know, deadline pressure. And I was young.'

'Young, yep I remember that.'

'Well…so she, this girl in the library, stops sneezing and her mouth just falls open, drops open like a drawbridge…and that hum…the electrical hum from the film…starts to come out of her mouth. This girl is sitting there in the library—pretty busy it was too—with her mouth open, salivating in some kind of trance, humming this…inhuman hum. I was waiting for subtitles to appear. It felt like it was just me and her, frozen in space and time.'

'Shit. What did you do?'

'Same as when my dad transformed into Beacham, I ran. I picked up my stuff and ran. I tried to convince myself that it just didn't happen, you know, that it was stress, lack of sleep, too much caffeine.'

'Did you see her again? The humming girl?'

'Yes, actually, I saw her a few days later. She was so nice. She asked if I was okay. What freaked you? she asked. I couldn't tell her that it was her. She said that she ran after me but that I was out of sight pretty quickly. I asked her if she remembered making a weird noise. She said that she remembered sneezing a lot but that was it.'

'Fuck.'

'Indeed.'

'So, back to the *raison d'être*. What do you think it wants, Katherine? Does it want to play with our minds? drive us—

pardon the pun—crazy? kill us…because—I dunno?—we witnessed something we shouldn't have?'

'I don't know, all good questions but…I don't know. It just, well…is. It exists and like a virus it seems to be able to adapt and survive…and…'

Katherine looked down at the dregs at the bottom of her cup. She tilted the cup back and forth, side to side, momentarily lost.

'I don't know if there is an antidote. But, look, what I will say is—and hopefully I'm not tempting fate here —but, I think there is something…benign about it. I don't think it's… a killer.'

'Hold on, Katherine. Benign! Poor old Frank gets pins and needles that virtually cripple him, twelve people get nosebleeds in the cinema, my girlfriend gets one—a nosebleed—a girl in the library makes inhuman sounds in your general direction, your dad becomes Beacham and I've just seen a waitress turn into Margot Kidder and back again. And…I'm sure you've got plenty of other, you know…*Driveshaft* stories—'

'I could write a book…or make a film.'

'You should. But, benign, I don't buy. I can't. I'm all over the place, at the moment. I don't know what is going to pop up or pop out or…so, benign just doesn't square with me, no offence.'

She didn't look offended, just thoughtful.

'Look, I'm not saying it isn't unnerving and…and I don't mean to muddy the waters between fiction and reality even more…but, it's not like that film *Ring* where a dark force goes out of its way to terrify its audience to death.'

'No…and, unlike *Ring*, this is real. Well, at least I think so. I mean, is it?'

'Real?'

'Yeah.'

'I guess…I mean, on some level. It was real last night when you were with Frank, wasn't it? And, real just now when, Lisa, the waitress was Margot Kidder for a couple of minutes. And Lena's nosebleed?'

'Yeah, well…there's a nasty stain on my favourite t-shirt.'

'There you go.'

Katherine tilted back in her seat, looked up at the ceiling.

'Okay, here we go. You're going to think this is bizarre, maybe weirder than all of the weird stuff you've been experiencing.'

'Now, you are scaring me.'

'Look, I think…I think—'

'Go on, I can't be more freaked than I am at the moment, can I?'

'Okay, I think it wants our help.'

We looked at each other. If you'd walked in and seen us at that moment you might have sighed, and thought we were deeply in love but, I was just mesmerised by her idea.

'Help? How can we help it, Katherine?'

'I don't know, Ben.' She looked down. She seemed to be slowly losing energy. 'Sorry, Ben. I haven't got past that thought. It's just stuck up here.' She tapped her index finger against her forehead. Then she seemed to reboot. 'So—I know it's a departure—but how did you and Lena meet?'

I was about to launch into mine and Lena's convoluted romance when I thought of the bloody t-shirt and felt a sudden jolt of concern for Lena, just as I did at Frank's the night before. I stood up quickly.

'Look, Katherine, no offence but I've really got to go. I'm sorry. I'm really worried about Lena. I haven't seen her in a while. I'm going to dash. Do you mind? I'll be in touch.'

Katherine stood, looked worried.

'I'm sorry, Ben. Was that too personal?'

'No, no, I'll tell you all about it one day…I'm just worried about her…worried about Lena. That's all. I haven't seen her since…sorry…can you pay? My treat next time.'

'Yes…that's fine. Go ahead. And remember, Ben…pinch of salt.'

I paused at the threshold of the café door, half in, half out, a coldness tingling away in my lower regions. I was going to tell her that they were also Frank's parting words to me last night. But, I figured, that she probably already knew.

Lena in the Frame

So, *Driveshaft* was officially omnipresent and perhaps omniscient. A cinematic virus? a celluloid bug? a filmic hallucinogen? Whatever the hell it was, its miasma had seeped into my conscious and unconscious worlds. It seemed determined to make cinematic theatre out of the lives of those who had experienced it—and even those who hadn't: Lisa/Margot, Angela, the irksome teens on the stairs, Katherine's dad, various squeaky doors, etcetera, etcetera. How did Katherine put it? It messes with the viewer's fantasy/reality receptors. You can say that again—whatever that means.

When I left Katherine, I immediately dropped the pinch of salt at the café door and replaced it with large helpings of panic and fear, chiefly about Lena's well-being. I thought of all of the potential *Driveshaft* scenarios: nosebleeds, pins and needles or perhaps just needles—full of her blood. Lena was not always phone friendly so I couldn't reach her that way. I left her a message: *Hi Lena, phone me.* It was short and sweet; I didn't want to worry her.

It's an aside, but a relevant one: Lena and I tried living together but we got on one another's tits very easily. One time, after an argument, she de-alphabetised my record collection. It was the final straw. We managed just over a year. Lena moved back in with her oldest friend, Stevie, whilst I stayed in my two-bedroom flat just up the road. We got on better this way. It sort of worked.

I rang the bell at Lena's place and Stevie answered. Stevie did everything languidly, she even managed to open the door languidly.

'Hey, Stevie, okay? Is Lena in?'

'Hey, Ben. I don't know… I mean, no. She left about an hour ago, said she was off to do some scrubbing, or something like that. You okay? You look kinda like that dude in that Scream painting.'

'Thanks, Stevie. I'm fine. You?' I was shuffling from foot to foot.

'Yeah, I've been worse.'

Stevie took a long, languid puff on her cigarette.

'Anyway, I thought it was you who picked her up.'

'Picked her up!'

'Yeah, I thought it was weird…because you…well, you don't drive, do you?'

'Drive!'

'Yeah…I didn't want to mention it because I thought that…you know…that Lena—'

'Might be having an affair?'

'Yeah…something like that.'

'Well, I hope she is.'

'What?'

'Nothing. Anyway, what did the car look like?'

'Oh, I don't know, I'm crap at cars…big, blue, noisy.'

I turned on my heel and thanked Stevie. She shouted after me, but I didn't hear what she said. I made it all the way back to mine at running-for-the-bus pace. I stumbled up the stairs, dropped my keys and smashed into the table. I heard an odd noise from the kitchen. I dashed into the kitchen and saw Lena scrubbing something over the sink.

'Alright, fuck-face…what's the rush? Trying to get the blood out of your fucking tee-shirt.'

'Thank fuck…you're here'.

'Yep…I've still got a key…remember?'

'No…I mean…you're here.'

I ran to Lena and squeezed her tightly.

'What the fuck! Are you high?'

'No, it's just that…I thought…'

I couldn't help myself, I burst out crying. Lena led me to the couch. I felt like a lost kid.

'Holy Christ! Three years together and you haven't cried once…hold on…there was that time at Christmas at the end of *The Wizard of Oz*…but apart from that you—'

'I went round to your flat…Stevie…she said that you had gone off…in a big…blue car and…I thought.'

'What?'

I laughed and blew my nose.

'So, you thought…no, you didn't. Tell me you didn't.'

Lena's expression managed to quickly shift from concern to incredulity, then amusement.

'Ha! You thought…you thought I'd been kidnapped by that car…the *Driveshaft* car and that it was sucking away at my blood?'

'I—'

'You, enormous prick. Drop this weirdness. It really is fucking with you.'

'But…but Stevie saw it, heard it.'

'Fuck Stevie, she's probably as high as a kite. You know her.'

'Yeah, but—'

'Look, I didn't go off in any phantom car, feel this, I'm here.'

Lena held out her arm. I felt it. It felt real.

'Satisfied? I left work, came over here because I felt bad about your stupid t-shirt, got the Vanish out and started scrubbing away, as is my wont.'

Lena started ringing out my t-shirt over the sink.

'So, what was, what did Stevie—'

'Fuck knows, she's a…a watchacallit…an enigma, an idiot savant.'

Lena smiled her saucy smile. Slid my soggy t-shirt over the kitchen radiator.

'You know what you need don't you? You know, to take your mind off stuff?'

I normally caught on but I was lost in a fog. Lena smiled her saucy smile again.

'Oh.'

'Lena, you're absolutely fucking ravenous lately.'

'I know, you're not wrong, I fucking am as well. I'm not sure what's—hey, are you complaining?'

'No, but, I'm not sure if I can get…excited, you know, after that shock.'

We both looked down at Lena's hand which was stroking my modesty.

'Oh.'

It was half past three in the morning—which morning I wasn't quite sure. I reached over to Lena but her side of the bed was cold and empty.

'Lena?'

My voice was swallowed by the dark room.

'Lena?'

It was raining hard again. Underneath the rain was a tapping sound. I slid out of bed, headed towards the sound. Lena was sitting at the kitchen table looking at the laptop, head very still, neck craned towards the screen. I folded my arms to my chest against the cold.

'Lena? It's half past three in the morning.'

Lena didn't answer. Just sat very still and stared at the screen. Then she looked up and turned her head my way. Her expression was blank. Lena but not Lena. It was as if she were asleep with her eyes open. My sphincter tightened and I froze.

'Lena…Lena are you—'

I couldn't finish the line. She just stared. I tried to move towards her but my feet were stuck to the cold floor.

'Lena, what the fuck are you doing? Wake up, Leen, please. This is weird.'

Lena continued to stare. She didn't blink.

'Shit, Lena, this is, what?…what is this?'

I tried to move again but no good. I felt the faintest electrical buzz in the air. Then heard the low, throbbing hum; the *Driveshaft* hum.

Lena was still just staring, vacant and elsewhere as the hum gradually got louder. Then her mouth fell open and she started to salivate from both sides of her mouth.

'Lena…that's not a good look. Wake the fuck up, Leen.'

I thought of Katherine's story about the girl in the library. A cold surge shivered through my balls. I almost evacuated.

'Lena. Stop. Wake up.'

The hum grew louder until it drowned out the rain. I tried to move again but no good. Stuck.

'Fuck. Lena. Wake up.'

The hum snapped to a dead stop. Then silence. I walked forward. Lena blinked, the light came back into her eyes and she closed her mouth, all at the same time.

'Research of course, dummy. I'm doing research. Why the fuck are you naked? It's about two degrees. You look terrible.'

I tried to speak but nothing came out. Lena stood, walked towards me and embraced me.

'Fuck, this business is doing your head in, baby'.

'But…don't you know what just happened?'

'Yeah, I told you. I'm doing research.'

I was dumbstruck and didn't have the energy to tell Lena that she'd just been possessed.

'What…what are you…were you researching?'

'The film of course. Trying to help you. Calm you down, you know'.

Lena took my hand. Now I felt like an old man being led back to bed in a care home.

'Hold on, can I see it?'

'See what?'

'Your research.'

What Day Is It?

Boy, did it click on, zoom past, full steam ahead, chug, chug. It was as if I was in that out of control car, hitting 140 mph on the desert highway. I was sure it was Tuesday but yesterday felt like Friday. And if it was Tuesday why was Katherine not working when I rang her? Why was she always available? Then it didn't seem to matter. Why worry about details like that when we were all trapped inside some alternate filmic universe?

I phoned Katherine that morning and told her about Lena being possessed by the *Driveshaft* hum.

'I'm sorry, Ben. Maybe it wouldn't have happened if I hadn't have told you about the girl in the library. It seems to be upping its game. Getting more and more inventive.'

'Upping its game sounds about right. You know, all of the hair on my body stood up. I didn't know that that could actually happen, but it did…it can.'

I heard the tiniest guffaw.

'I'm so sorry, Ben. Is Lena okay?'

'Yeah, just scared the crap out of me. She blanked it out, like your girl in the library, she hadn't a clue that it had happened. Just said that she felt tired. Said that I freaked her out, standing there with the weirdest look on my face, naked as the day I was born.'

'What was she researching?'

'The film, apparently. Said she couldn't sleep. Said she wanted to find out where it was shot. Which is all a bit odd because she says—or said—she didn't give a fuck about the film. Thinks I should drop the whole business, but she keeps stoking it, you know.'

'Sounds like it's gotten hold of her too.'

'Yeah, she's succumbing to its…benignity.'

'Sorry, wish I'd never said that either.'

'Where was it shot, anyway?'

'Well, Margot and Beacham both say New Mexico, so…I'm guessing there's something in that.'

'Right…anyway, Lena's research turned up something that you'll want to see.'

'Go on.'

'Well, she had this website up about Dungeness.'

'Dungeness? Dungeness, Kent? Dungeness, power station, Dungeness?'

'Yeah, all of those. She used to go there a lot as a kid. That was where she used to get nosebleeds.'

I'm sure I heard Katherine sit up.

'I see. Now that is very interesting.'

'Well…yeah. I think you should come and see for yourself.'

Katherine did come and see. She was over too quickly it seemed to me. Like she'd been waiting downstairs or something. Then they were both—Katherine and Lena—warming their hands in front of the hot lap-top, tapping and flicking and pointing, oohing and aaaahing.

Lena was taking Katherine through some of the images she'd discovered the night before.

'So, what do you think?'

'It's…well, freakish. Just so alike, even that road there…look. Great work, Lena. But, what's the —'

Lena, buzzing from coffee and a lack of sleep, ignored Katherine and ploughed on.

'Yeah… erm…FF tells me I was in some kind of trance, making a weird noise. But, between me and you, Kat, I think he's cracking…this sabbatical…his mind has wandered way off limits. Some people need work to keep it together, you know, maintain boundaries.'

Katherine smiled but she slowed Lena down with her calm. We all supped our coffee. Katherine was subtle and probing.

'It was curious though… about your flatmate seeing you go off in a car. Have you asked her about it, Lena?'

'No, she's gone AWOL. She's always doing it…on a permanent sabbatical is Stevie.'

Katherine leaned in closer towards the laptop. She was whizzing through the images of Dungeness.

'Yeah, Ben tells me you've been having weird shit going on for how long, Kat?'

'Thirty years, virtually.'

'Virtually is, I think, the best word.'

'Ooh! How astute, Right on the money there, FF.'

'Ah, you've got pet initials for him. That's so sweet.'

Lena smirked and raised her eyebrows. 'Yeah, isn't it.'

Katherine took a gulp of coffee and then sprayed it back into Lena's, Keep Calm or Fuck Off, mug.

'Oh, my god…look…look at this.'

Katherine wiped her mouth and the sides of the mug before she put it down. The three of us swore in unison at what was before us on the screen. The image that Katherine had enlarged was of a one-storey building with four enormous blacked out windows, two either side of a set of metallic doors. On top of the flat roof were two satellite dishes.

'Oh my god! What?…so, hold on…I'm baffled. So, the film was actually shot in Dungeness? This fucking place, from the film, is actually in Dungeness, Kent? Is it?'

'No, no…what this is Lena, is an invitation.' Katherine did a first-class dramatic pause. 'And, I think we'd better accept it.'

I grabbed my mobile phone and stalked off into the kitchen.

'Where you off to?'

'Hello, Frank?'

Four, Possessed

Frank was standing outside his front door, looking up at the rain, when we got there. He seemed ready for action. He looked younger but, even in the cold light of day, still resembled Beacham. I did the introductions. We were, of course, drenched. Frank invited us in and got out his ever-ready golden liquor. We moved some furniture so we could all sit comfortably. We sat. We all accepted a whisky; partly for the warmth, but mostly for the shock.

'Did you see the freaky teens on the stairs, Benny?'

'No, no sign of them today, Frank.'

There was a comfort that seemed to envelop us, like we'd survived some trauma a long time ago and had met up again to heal one another. Katherine and Frank reminisced, told us all about their *Driveshaft* moments or 'greatest hits' as Frank called them. It was strange but I almost felt slightly envious as they trawled through their otherworldly experiences. Me and Lena were *Driveshaft* amateurs in comparison. Frank's accent was mostly South London but did keep slipping into the Southern States. Lena ended a lengthy but not uncomfortable lull in the conversation.

'Well, I think Frank wins…I mean imagine losing total control of your car and then the seat-belt starts to try and throttle you? Lord, I bet you thought those syringes were going to pop out, didn't you, Frankie?'

'Yep, tell the truth, Lena. I thought my number was up, darlin'.'

Frank sat forward in his chair, finished his whisky and sighed an enormous sigh. Frank's soft authority seemed to bring us together. We were a cult, with Frank at the helm. We were waiting for his declamation. He cleared his throat.

'So…okay…time for action, folks…I guess. We've all been infected or injected or possessed or we're being cursed or haunted or taunted or whatever. And, well, I'll speak for myself here, but it—'

Frank hesitated to say the name.

'Shit, maybe we should call it the American film, like the Scottish play, ya know. Anyway, *Driveshaft*, seemed to be at bay for a while. Ya know, I've had a connection with it since that night at the Ritzy in eighty-eight, and its visits have been sporadic at best. I used to have maybe half a dozen episodes a year…but…it feels like it's getting bored and has made itself a bit of a nuisance lately…upped its game so ta speak, 'specially since Benny here contacted me.'

'Shit, Frank, I'm sorry.'

I looked down at my hands.

'Don't feel bad, Benny. I'm getting pins and needles regular now and it ain't funny, but it ain't your fault either, buddy. And, I got them bastard kids outside making so many of the weird noises from the soundtrack and reciting lines from the movie on a fucking loop. And, worst of all I keep slipping into this cartoon American accent at the drop of a fucking hat.'

It was a decent line. Lena laughed the loudest. She liked Frank a lot. Think it was a father thing.

'Yep, that is easily the worst symptom, Frankie.'

'Symptoms? Nice way a puttin' it, Lena darlin'. Frank nodded sagely. He was gradually starting to sound more like Beacham. 'Seems that you've had some symptoms yourself, darlin'.'

'Well, I had a nosebleed the other night and according to…FF over there, I was also humming in a trance. But—as I told Kat, I think he might be cracking.'

I nodded and tried a smile.

'And, don't forget, Stevie,' I said.

Lena snapped. 'No, do forget, Stevie.'

Frank and Katherine looked interested.

'Stevie?'

I piped up. 'Yeah, she's Lena's flatmate. Stevie saw Lena being whisked off in a noisy blue car.'

'And, I take it that Stevie hasn't seen *Driveshaft*?' Katherine asked.

'Yeah, I mean…no…that's the thing.'

Katherine turned to Frank. They both looked grave.

'That's…unusual, I'd say. What do you think Frank?'

'Dunno…guess so but, like I said, it's getting stronger.'

Katherine nodded. 'Yes, that's what I thought.'

'Christ! It's becoming air-borne,' said Lena.

'Well, like I say, I'm having more episodes since Ben…erm, surfaced.'

'Thanks, Frank.'

'Yeah, he's a bit like—what?…herpes? shingles?'

'Thanks, Leen.'

'So, why Dungeness, Lena darlin'?'

'I…I don't know, Frankie. I was looking for stuff on the film, you know, to help out Benny. And, it just up and popped into my head and before I knew it, I was drowning in images of the fucking place. And memories. I just got carried away. I was really tired, but my fingers just kept, you know, doing the walking…and next thing I know…FF grabs me, tells me I'm in a trance.'

'You were, Lena.'

I turned to Frank and Katherine who exchanged a quick but meaningful look.

'She was.'

Frank, interlaced his fingers and looked gravely at Lena.

'Memories, what memories, Lena darlin'?'

'Well, I used to go there—to Dungeness, I mean—as a kid. I had these nosebleeds and…'

Lena paused. Her face was suddenly ashen.

'Shit, I'm in it…aren't I? I'm in it up to here.' Her hand was hovering above her head, shaking. 'Fuck, I feel sort of heavy and light and dizzy and…weird. Think it's that fucking whisky, Frankie.'

Frank looked worried. We all did.

'I think you know it's not the whisky, darlin'.'

'Crap.'

Lena held her head, rubbed her temples.

'Crap'.

Katherine snuggled up close to Lena on Frank's two-seater couch. 'It's okay, Lena. Let it out.'

'Crap.'

Lena started to tremble and moan.

'Crap.'

'Benny, see to ya girl, I'm gonna go get some water.'

I knelt before Lena, held both her hands in mine.

'It's okay, Leen. It's okay, baby.'

'It's not, you know…I'm fucking unravelling.'

Frank came back with a large glass of water for Lena.

'Here ya go, Lena darlin'. Sip up.'

Lena took the glass and swallowed quickly, started to cough. Red in the face, laughing and coughing.

'Oh god, sorry everybody. Shame on me, I'm ashamed…deeply. Fuck, feel like I need to be exorcised.'

That's when a sweet but heavy presence filled the room. We all felt it. It was something we always brought up for years afterwards. We paused and just looked at one another with this weight floating around us. Then, Lena broke the spell and jumped up. I flinched as she shouted.

'That's it, that's fucking it'.

Lena left a long pause as we looked up. She was in a sort of Bruce Lee pose.

'Exorcism, we need to perform an exorcism. That's what we need to perform, right? Am I right? Kat? Frank? fuck-face?'

Katherine raised her eyebrows, sat forward in her chair. She looked impressed, almost dumbstruck. And it was—I think—the first time I'd heard her swear.

'Fuck, you know, I think that might well…be…it…the help, the help that it needs. Yes, an exorcism. It's a horror film which is itself sort of possessed and, in turn, has sort of possessed us, its…viewers. So…yes…an exorcism. I've never…Lena, you are a genius.'

Lena looked proud of herself. Smiled at me smugly. Then her face dropped.

'Okay, but how the fuck do we exorcise a fucking film?'

There was a long pause. Outside, the rain carried on regardless. We all sort of looked around the room, non-plussed. Then something seemed to wink at me. I looked down at the side of my chair. And there was the book I'd seen the other night—last night? the night before?—*Easy Riders, Raging Bulls*.

'Fuck.' I stood up, waving the book in the air. 'That's it. This is it. I've got it.' I held it up like a trophy. I opened the front page and showed Frank the message that Big Ben wrote him.

Hey Franklin,
Here's to a happy ending, bud.
Too much love.
Big Ben (Xmas 98) x

Frank smiled warmly. Passed the book over to Katherine. Katherine smiled and passed the book to Lena. I stood breathing heavily. It was Lena's turn to smile but she didn't. She frowned and swore.

'What the…sorry but I'm not getting it. Who the fuck is Big Ben?'

Frank patted Lena's arm. Showed her the message in the book again.

'He's an old friend, Lena…was a beautiful man but it's this line about the happy ending, Lena darlin', it's all about the happy ending.'

'Okay, Frank, that sounds wrong, and anyway that film has the least happy ending I've—' Lena screwed up her face. 'Fuck me. You mean that's the exorcism? We pretend that there was a happy ending—to the film?'

'I think we need to go a little further than that, Lena.'

Frank leapt up, headed for the kitchen. He returned with the whisky bottle again and refilled our glasses. We clinked the glasses, raised them and, at the same time, almost sang:

Happy Ending.

The Shit Brown Volvo

Again, time went into full warp speed. Before I knew it me and Lena were outside Frank's place, next morning. Can't remember the day or the time, but it was early. It was drizzling but not enough so that we needed to take shelter. Lena was in playful mood. Too playful.

'Hey, leave that alone, Leen. It needs a rest, you know. What's got into you? Since we watched *Driveshaft* you've been—'

'I know, I'm just gagging for it, all the time.'

'Yeah, what do you suppose has got into you?'

Lena smiled archly, resisted the obvious gag.

'Fuck, I dunno, maybe it's an aphrodisiac. I'll have to ask Kat.'

'Lena, please don't. Katherine's—'

'Katherine's what? Too sophisticated to talk about shagging. I bet she's a proper slut.'

Just as Lena said this Katherine pulled around the corner in, what can only be described as, a shit brown Volvo.

'Holy fuck, that is class. Look at that shitheap.' Lena bounced up to Katherine's car as she parked up. 'You're not going to ask me to drive, Kat, or look in the boot, are you?'

Katherine laughed.

Lena leaned in the driver's window as Katherine cut the engine. 'Oh, wow, Kat, I love these cars. They are so fucking ugly.'

'Thanks, Lena.'

Lena paused and reached into her Columbo style trench-coat pocket and fished out a pack of cigarettes. Katherine got out of the car.

'Where's Frank?'

I shook my head.

'Don't know, shall we pop up and knock?'

Lena puffed away. Offered a cigarette to Katherine. Katherine took one, to my surprise.

'So, Kat, can I ask you a personal question?'

'Sure, go ahead, Lena.'

'You know this whole *Driveshaft* thing?'

'Yes.'

'Holy fuck. Would you look at him?'

I was very glad to see Frank, even though what he was wearing seemed to be, well, asking for trouble. It meant that Lena didn't have a chance to ask Katherine about *Driveshaft* being a potential aphrodisiac.

'It's a beauty Franklin,' said Lena. 'I love it.'

'Thanks, darlin'. I kinda figured that, you know, in for a penny…'

'Right on. Now that's the spirit, Frankie.'

'Benny, you don't look so sure, buddy.'

'Frank, I think it's a touch of class.'

Frank took off his white Stetson, waved it in the air and shouted.

'Let's hit the fuckin' road. Actually, scrap that…just gimme a hand with this will ya, someone?'

Lena dropped her cigarette, walked over to Frank and took the blue IKEA bag he was struggling with.

'Christ, weighs a fucking ton. Whose body's in here, Frank?'

'Glad you asked, Lena darlin'. This in here is the answer, the key, the holy water of this particular exorcism, folks.'

Lena peered into the bag and pulled out a first-aid dummy and a tiny pair of wooden steps. 'Everyone…meet Charlie.'

Katherine smiled. 'Ah, I've pumped a few of those during my time, pardon the phrase…you know for workplace first aid.'

'Yep, Charlie is gonna help save our asses.'

'Asses! Arses, Frank! You mean arses. And the tiny wooden steps?'

'Cap'n Birdseye, of course.'

'Que?'

'We need 'em for those high old birds-eye view shots and the chopper POVs. Remember?'

'Ah. Okay. Low flying bird.'

'Anyway, sorry, y'all…I mean everyone…but I just have no control over it, the accent.'

Lena dropped Charlie into the boot. Frank hobbled around to the passenger side. I opened the door.

Katherine winced as she watched Frank struggle into the car.

'Bad today, Frank?'

'Bad enough, Kat.'

We were all in the car. Katherine spoke to me and Lena whilst looking at us from the rear-view mirror.

'Okay, erm, so me and Frank have been tightening the plan. Frank, do you want to—'

'No, Katherine, go ahead, you're better at this talking business. I'll just ramble.'

'Okay. Erm…give me a sec. Wait till I'm on the south circular. Everybody belted up? Stupid question.'

Nobody had.

'It's the law after all.'

'I think we can call these exceptional circumstances, Katherine.'

Lena was a little blunter.

'I don't know about you lot but I am sitting on this fucking belt all the way there. I am taking no chances.'

'And if the police pull us over.'

'Then we tell them the truth. What is the truth by the way?'

Lena leaned forward, frowned. 'Okay…Frank?'

'Lena?' Frank turned.

'Tell me that you don't have a pair of scissors in your hand, Frankie.'

Frank went quiet.

'Frank, let me put it another way. Show me what the fuck you have in your hand, please?'

Frank held up a huge pair of black handled scissors. Lena clapped her hands and laughed.

'Look, you never know, do you? I mean, we don't know if that belt is gonna…I dunno, spring into life and throttle poor Katherine there, do we?'

Lena winked at Frank. 'We sure don't, pardner.'

The Road to Dungeness

Dungeness is about seventy-five miles from Frank's place. We guessed it would take roughly two hours. During the journey there was, at times, a palpable sense of dread. It felt as if the sum of all of our *Driveshaft* experiences fluttered around the inside of the car on dark wings. Katherine was soon on the south circular. And before anybody got a chance to say a word the rain started.

'Got to have broken all previous records, hasn't it?'

'Rain?'

'Rain.'

Lena said this as she stroked the zip of my jeans. I pulled her hand away and glared at her.

Katherine was grinning at us—on and off—in the rear-view mirror, like an amused parent keeping an eye on her naughty kids. She cleared her throat.

'Okay, so, as I was saying earlier, Frank and I have done some tightening…and, please bear in mind that this can change…you know, if you don't agree, okay Lena? Ben?'

'Wow, you and Frank have got pretty cosy.'

'Yep, well, we're veterans, Lena darlin', ya know.'

'Okay, Kat. Fire away.'

'Well, we had you down as our Margot, Lena. You are, clearly, the obvious candidate.'

'Thanks, a compliment, I guess. So, I'm going to be—what?—strapped into the car and have my blood sucked? Is that the deal?'

Frank laughed nervously. 'No, no…no, it's all a simulation, ya see.'

'Simulation?'

Katherine turned slightly towards us before she focussed on the road again.

'Yeah, simulation, the same as we can't afford to go to New Mexico. We can't afford to hire a film crew. We can't afford—'

'Very much?'

'Yes, you've got it,' said Katherine.

Frank carried on. 'So…we are going to respect it…the spirit of the film…and create our own ending out of the resources we have.'

'Shit, sounds like the *A-Team*, Frank.'

'Yeah, well I hope this particular plan comes together, ya know.'

Katherine carried on. 'So, anyway, our main resource is our good will and respect towards the… force that is alive inside, and outside, *Driveshaft*. And our willingness to…well, believe in it and…work with it in order to put an end to the thing properly, you know, the film…and the—'

'Curse?'

'Didn't want to say it but, okay…curse.'

Lena's voice had some edge to it. 'So, how will the film know that you…we mean well? I can't believe I just said that by the way.'

'We don't know.'

'Pandora's box, Lena'.

'Come again?'

'Hope is all that we have, darlin'.'

Lena was half-drowsing, her head on my shoulder. 'Are we there yet?'

Katherine looked into the rear-view mirror again. 'About half-hour, I'd guess.'

Katherine's windshield wipers were working overtime. The steady rhythm had sent me half off into a fuzzy zone full of *Driveshaft* miscellany.

Lena elbowed me. I sat up. She held up her phone.

'Okay, here's the inflight entertainment. Dungeness facts and figures. Ready?'

'Go for it, Lena darlin'.'

'Okay, well, for starters…the Pilot pub looks great—they do the best fish and chips in the world—according to them. Will we go there?'

'Bad idea, Lena.'

'Yeah, I'm with Frank,' I said. Pubs in horror movies? Generally a no-no.'

'Yeah… oh, what's it called. The pub in the werewolf film with the Americans? Oh, shit…'

' The Slaughtered Lamb? *American Werewolf in London*.'

'Asshole…I mean, arsehole. Okay, get this…some folk refer to Dungeness as the only desert in the UK owing to limited rainfall—Christ that'll be a blessing—and its barren landscape. Some people, however, poo-poo this idea. They say it's bollocks and is a line for the tourists.'

'Figures.'

Lena narrowed her eyes at her phone.

'And get this…there is a unique zone in Dungeness known as the boil or the patch which is loved by anglers. The hot waste-water from the nuclear power station means that there is a very rich diversity of fish here. Fuck me, nuclear water. I bet they've pulled a few two-headed creatures out of there.'

Lena sat up. Banged her head on the Volvo's ceiling.

'Fuck, they're the tallest fuckers in Europe yet they skimp on headroom…the Swedes, I mean. Anyway, do you think that nuclear waste caused the weirdness in *Driveshaft*? You know was somehow transmitted through the film because Dungeness looks so similar to New Mexico and, then…we all got some kind of—'

There was a heavy silence. Lena cleared her throat.

'Okay, I'll move on. Anyway, the hot waste-water encourages seabirds from miles around.'

'Picking out those two-headed critters, no doubt, Lena darlin'.'

'Wow, get this. There are over six hundred types of plant found in Dungeness. This is roughly a third of those found in Britain. Weird, I thought there would be like hundreds of thousands of them, you know, plants.'

Lena was getting restless. We were all feeling the tension the closer we got to Dungeness.

'Any chance of whacking the radio on, Katherine?' I asked.

Katherine looked at all of us in turn. 'Erm…Frank. What do you think?'

'No way. Sorry, Benny, just doesn't seem…you know, appropriate.'

'Yeah, double F, not appropriate. Holy fuck!'

Lena was looking at her phone, mouth wide open.

'What's up?'

'Well, according to this encyclopaedic website a French interpretation of Dungeness is…dangerous nose.'

Frank laughed. 'Wow, nice connection.'

'Bastard place, bastard film, bastard nose.' Lena snuggled up to me and went very quiet.

Katherine looked in the rear-view mirror. 'Probably to do with the geography of the place, you know, sticking out on the coast.'

'Yeah, lots of lighthouses there, baby. That's what the dangerous nose reference is.'

'Shut up…bastards.'

We did.

We travelled on in silence. Katherine's wipers must have been exhausted. Frank was snoring from the passenger seat. Lena was mumbling in her sleep and dribbling a little. I didn't tell her this. In front of us, the clouds were parting and a low and bright November sun welcomed us to Dungeness.

'Be a rainbow soon.'

Frank mumbled and sat up. 'Wassat?'

'Rainbow, Frank. Sun and rain.'

Frank was stretching when he suddenly yelled, 'What the fuck!'

'What is it? Pins and needles, Frank?'

'No…no, look. Kat, pull over. Look, everyone…side a the road, back there…pull over…LOOK!'

Lena and I gasped simultaneously as we saw Eve at the side of the road, running towards the car, waving her arms above her head.

Lena grabbed Katherine's arm.

'No…drive on Katherine, for fuck's sake. It's too weird.'

Eve shouted and waved at the car as we flew past her.

Katherine slowed the car down. 'We can't…leave her…it's our duty. We've got to follow the rules. Besides it's pissing down. The poor kid is soaked.'

'She's not even real, is she? So, how the fuck can she be soaked?'

'Well, let's find out.'

Eve was soaked, grateful and very believable. I opened my door to let her in.

'Oh…lord, thank you so much. You've saved my life…you really have. I knew somethin' good would happen when that rainbow come.'

Eve squeezed in beside me as I squeezed Lena over to the door. Eve felt real. Wet and warm. She never really made eye contact with any of us. It was as if she were cut adrift in her own space which, of course, *technically*, she was. Frank turned around, beamed at Eve. She was miles away and only responded when somebody spoke to her.

'Where ya goin, darlin'?'

'I'm going to LA. Are you going that way?'

Lena was about to say something when I elbowed her.

Frank's voice was deep and soothing. 'Yeah, matter of fact, we are on the way there right now. We can take you all the way downtown. Sorry, what's your name, darlin'?'

'Eve, hi I'm Eve.'

'Hi Eve, I'm Frank, the driver here is Katherine and in back with ya there is Benny and Lena.'

We all said hi, back and forth. Then Eve became still and mute, stared ahead in a trance.

Frank whispered, 'I think we need to, ya know, lead her…erm, bring her out some, ya know.'

Lena whispered violently. 'Holy Christ Frank, she'll hear you.'

'I don't think she can at the moment. I think she's…'

'A robot? Is it like *Westworld*?'

'No, no…nothing like that…well, somethin' like that. Remember, we're here to do a job, fulfil a quest…and Eve here is a part of our quest so we are in the box seat, so to speak, ya know? Her role is restricted…she's sorta stuck in a limbo between the celluloid and the real, whereas we…shit, I'm not sure I've got that right…erm…anyway…why don't you ask her a question, Lena darlin'?'

'Shit, Frank! That—'

'Fuck off, FF. I can be subtle.' Lena turned towards Eve's static form. 'Erm…hi Eve…how are you?'

Eve sprung to life. She started to blink, turned towards Lena and, as Lena put it later, looked right the fuck through me.

'Oh…I'm hurtin' so bad. My baby left me on the roadside, see…'

Eve froze again, tears slowly rolled down her cheeks.

'Great, well done, Leen.'

'What did I say?'

Suddenly, Eve whirred back into life and continued, looking straight at—or through—Lena.

'…we were going to LA together, to start fresh coz stuff round about where we lived was getting us so down and all…so we arranged to meet outside Ringo's—where I sometimes work—but…but when she came there, when Margot came to pick me up…she…just drove on…she wouldn't let me get in to the car. She just looked so scairt…I run after her but the car…the car was so fast…it was outta sight so quick…it threw up dirt and grit then it was gone and my baby was gone and I've been here waiting by this roadside forever and no one came…no one came 'cept you. I'm so grateful to y'all for stopping. You saved my life.'

There was a small beat and Eve switched off again. Lena waved her hand in front of Eve's eyes.

'Shit, she's gone again.'

I leaned towards Eve. Frank raised an eyebrow.

'Careful now, Benny. It…she's in a delicate frame, remember?'

'Sure, sure, Frank'.

Katherine half turned towards me although she was mostly talking to Frank.

'There are some plot gaps that it might be nice to…erm, have filled…if you know what I mean, Ben.'

'Yeah, like how the fuck did Margot kill the fat guy?'

'Yes, that was sort of what I had in mind, Lena.'

Frank looked concerned.

'Okay, Benny but just go easy, bud.'

'Frank, you've got a heart of gold, worried about this non-existent being.'

Lena started to feel Eve's face. 'Mind you she—feels like the real thing.'

'Lena, stop squeezing her face.'

'Sorry.'

'She's still got feelings, Lena. Look at that face. Those tears.' I cleared my throat. Felt really nervous. 'Hi Eve.'

Eve jerked back into life. 'Oh, hi…how ya doin'?'

'Fine thanks, Eve? I just wanted to ask what it was that was getting you down. You said that you wanted to start fresh because stuff was getting you down?'

'Yeah, Lord, that town, the whole town was…kinda cursed, ya know. The juice kep' failing and the cars kep' breaking and the people were getting sick…nose bleeds, bad stuff had gotten into their blood. Some folk said it was the military, some said it was radiation, some said it was some kinda curse was makin' it happen. I dunno but we, Margot and me, just needed to get out. We were getting stale and sick, we weren't eating well and it was cold and dark allathe time. And…and also my daddy he…he just was all the time on at Margot…he was her boss, ya know…and he didn't like us bein together. He was a…just a mean old man…so my baby, she used her…her gift. The gift she brought from the place she's from, the other place. She used that gift to kill my daddy.'

You could hear the collective gasp and our jawbones almost detaching. Katherine nearly crashed the car. She swerved off to the left in the driving rain. Eve 'shut down' after the revelation. Nobody could speak for a while, even Lena. Eventually it was Lena who spoke.

'Holy fuck, so, she got her baby…she got Margot to bump off her…daddy?'

'Lena, ease up, girl. Remember, it's only a movie. None of it actually happened, darlin'.'

'You're right, Frank…but it feels real right now. Like somebody really died and somebody really killed them.'

'Is there anything else we want to find out? I mean, should we pump her some more? Or is that cruel?'

'Time to let her go, I say. She can't really give us anymore. Poor kid.'

'How do we let her go, Frank?'

'We tell her that we're here…in LA.'

'What? The last sign, if you didn't notice, said Romney Marsh, not Los Angeles.'

'I don't think she'll know or care, remember her status, she's like a conduit…here to aid us on our quest. She's not—'

'Real? She feels warm and she feels wet and…I don't get it.'

Lena looked upset for Eve. She seemed to have taken Eve's revelations literally. It was weird. But, then we all sort of believed in it. We all wanted to help her.

'None of us quite get it, Lena darlin'…but we're immersed in something beyond our ken. I'm not the rational centre of all of this. I can't play that role and explain it. It's happening…that's all I know…and I think we should let Eve go. Tell her we're in LA and that she'll soon be able to see Margot.'

'Frank's right, I think, maybe it's better to think that at the moment we are as much in her world as she is in ours.'

'So, we're sort of—what?—partially in a film?'

Frank and Katherine responded at the same time.

'Something like that.'

'Okay, Kat…look up yonder. Pull up at that petrol station and we'll tell Eve that this is it. This is downtown LA.'

'Oh, fuck this. What happened to your twenty-four-carat heart of gold, Frank? You just gave us the moral high ground about her having feelings and getting wet, now you want to drop her at a dodgy looking petrol station in the pissing rain in the middle of pissing Kent.'

Frank turned. It was the first time I'd seen anything close to anger on his face.

'You wanna adopt her, Lena? She can't come to Dungeness. It'll hex the…exorcism.'

Lena looked a little crestfallen. Katherine indicated and slowly eased into the petrol station. Frank apologised to Lena, then turned and looked earnestly at Eve.

'Say…Eve, baby?'

Eve sprung to life again, smiled her engaging but blank eyed smile in Frank's direction. 'Hi.'

'Guess what, Eve?'

'What's that now?'

'We're here. We're in LA.'

'No, oh my Lord…I…I better get out and find her. We're starting fresh, we're gonna do well in LA. Peopl'll like us in LA.'

'You'll find her. She won't be far. You'll be with Margot again, Eve. I just know you will, darlin'.'

'Thank y'all so much again…you saved my life.'

Eve was half way out of the car when she turned to Frank.

'You know, you look so familiar, sir. Do I know you?'

Frank's eyebrows almost left his head but he kept his cool.

'No, darlin', I've just got one of those faces, ya know.'

'Oh, okay. Anyway, thanks so much again.'

Eve kept thanking us as she stepped out of the car and then walked out into the rain and into god knows where.

'Shit, close one, Beacham.'

'Yeah.'

'Where the fuck did she go?'

'Good question.'

'Was she ever here?

'Good question.'

'So, if she was never here then I guess I shouldn't worry about where she's going…gone?'

'You got it, Lena.'

Dungeness was closer than we thought. The sun had gone, and dusk was starting to swallow the eerie bluish light. Katherine's shit-brown Volvo crept warily into Dungeness's majestic weirdness.

'This is it, all right. Feel that?'

We all felt it. We all nodded.

The Cheapest Film Shoot in History

To say that the *shoot* was low-key would be overstating it. It was the cheapest film in history—all six minutes of it. Katherine reckoned the budget was about fifty pounds, most of which was petrol money. It was a 'stand-in' job. Katherine's old battered, shit-brown Volvo stood in for the menacing blue and white Mustang. Katherine stood in for Eve; Lena for Margot. My cheap Sony video-camera stood in for a whole film crew. The only believable stand-ins were Frank, in his white Stetson, who did a near perfect voice-over job as Beacham for the radio, and, of course, the location. We couldn't afford New Mexico, we had Dungeness for our *Driveshaft* exorcism.

The actual reshoot itself was pretty unremarkable. To document it in detail would waste precious time, space and energy and would also serve as a spoiler. So, I won't. The *incidental* events and details, however, were important and worth spending some time over.

It was November, so it got dark at about half four. I felt that we needed to get the shoot done by then. Frank and Katherine, the cooler and wiser heads, were amused. Katherine looked like the archetypal director, hands on hips she gazed enigmatically into the 'desert' of Dungeness as she spoke.

'It doesn't matter about time or light or dark, Benny. As long as we make the offering. These gods aren't that particular. It doesn't matter if it's pitch black or Lena looks nothing like Margot, or the car can just make fifty miles an hour and it's brown instead of blue. What matters is that we are all here in this…zone together.'

Katherine's Volvo trundled up and down the main road through Dungeness as the afternoon dwindled. In our various stand in roles we performed our exorcism. Inevitably, we drew a crowd, the most conspicuous member of which was Sheriff Beale. It was obvious it was him. He stood apart from the other locals—the real ones who didn't seem to notice him—and looked, well, like a Sheriff. At first, he was impassive and rocklike. His arms were folded across his chest and there was dried blood in his beard and moustache. After a few minutes of his stony observation Sheriff Beale sauntered over. Lena smiled and walked towards him.

'Take it easy, Lena,' said Frank.

'I got this, Frank. Hold ya horses, partner.'

'Howdy Sheriff.'

Sheriff Beale chuckled an amiable chuckle.

'Howdy…I like that…I like you already, young lady.'

His voice was baritone, slow and bloody sexy. Lena almost swooned.

'Well…we like you too, Sheriff. You keep a clean and godly town, sir.'

'Ha-ha, well I do appreciate your…appreciation, young lady.'

Lena was flirting, as was the phantom Sheriff. She introduced us all and we all experienced the Sheriff's firm and ice-cold grip. He took off his large black Stetson and squinted at us.

'Hey, now, look…I just wanted to say that I'm awful glad you folks decided to come down here and perform this…service for our community. Lord knows we've had ourselves a time of it lately. So, on behalf of everybody hereabouts…ya know, all those who have at one time or another been involved in this…project…well we hope that the Lord looks out for ya coz you deserve his kindly eye upon ya. I won't be far away so, if you want anything and I do mean anything, you just yell…'specially you, little lady.'

'Thank you so much, Sheriff. We won't hesitate, ya hear'.

The Sheriff winked at Lena, chuckled and wandered off.

'Fuck me, Lena!'

'Oh, come on, she did just fine, Benny. Kinda green-eyed there, aincha buddy?'

'Well, he fucking well winked at her.'

'To be honest, I went off him when I touched his cold and clammy skin.'

'Seemed all right to me, did ole Sheriff Beale'

'Yeah, and a black Sheriff too. Pretty unusual for the times, no?'

We all looked at Lena.

Confusion floated in the air until Katherine spoke.

'What do you mean…black, Lena?'

'You're kidding right? He was black. A tall, middle-aged, handsome black man, clean shaven…razor-blade cheekbones, dried blood around his nose and mouth. And that voice.'

Frank chuckled. 'Well, I saw a full-blooded Navajo. Tall, skinny, bronze skin, and yeah…cheek bones like razor blades. And, yeah, blood around the nose. You Katherine?'

'Solid and chubby…looked a bit like Captain Kirk…William Shatner …and blood from the nose and down his, clean shaven, chin.'

'Benny?'

'James Brolin in his prime…tall, imposing, handsome, beard and tash covered in blood.'

'What the fuck? Four different Sheriff Beales?'

'Yes, makes perfect sense.'

'Go on then, Kat…spill.'

'Well, he wasn't actually in the film so how could we see the same Sheriff. We made him up from our imaginations. We each projected our own archetypal Sheriff.'

'Okay…but…why was he…you know, all there I mean, he talked to us and didn't switch off, like Eve did. Why?'

'I think he liked you so much Lena that he forgot the rules.'

'Anyway, you two are racists. Me and Frank are officially the most progressive. My Sheriff Beale was black, Frank's was an Indian.'

Lena and Frank *high fived*.

Then Frank got serious. Put his hands on his hips and looked up at the gathering dark clouds.

'Somebody gimme a hand to get Charlie, and the resta this stuff outta the boot?'

The shoot finished just as the clouds gathered. They seemed eager to shed their load. Frank had been struggling with his pins and needles and was sat in the Volvo's passenger seat with the door open, rubbing his legs. He was in full Beacham mode; voice and looks and verbal tics. Katherine and I were checking out the final few frames on my Sony cheap-cam when the camera ran out of juice. Katherine swore.

'Fuck, this is bad, according to your meter just now you should have lots of life left in the battery.'

Katherine jumped into the driver's seat. Lena and me leapt into the back. Frank kept his door open. Katherine tried to start the car but no luck.

'What! The tank is well over half full. Well, it was.'

Frank smiled wryly at Katherine.

'Oh, I get it, the juice! We've gone and run out of juice.'

'Ah…of course, Lena, you're right.'

Frank then jerked his thumb out towards the back windscreen. 'Was that there a minute ago?'

We ignored the rain and got out of the car drawn, like magnets, to what was before us. It shimmered away, surrounded by a pulsating orange light. Its ominous black windows beckoning and repelling us.

'Well, here we are…there it is. It's what we expected. It's gotta be done.'

'Who's going first?'

'Do we have to? We could squeeze into the car. The heating might still work.'

'Sorry, Lena. We have to go, darlin'.'

'Yeah but…I don't want to see that body, who we now know is Eve's dad, behind that fucking door. I mean, its, he's not in the film so going by the Sheriff Beale experience, I'm going to summon up something beyond fucking gruesome from my morbid imagination. Can we give it a miss?'

'We can't back off, Lena. Come on, it's our duty.'

'She's right, baby. We've got to.'

'Who's leading the way then?'

'Well, Frank, you look and sound totally like Beacham, so…'

Katherine walked towards the metallic doors which split the four large black windows. The doors squeaked when Katherine opened them. We followed her in; wet and expectant on the threshold.

Blackout.

'What the fuck.'

'Benny, where are you? Ben, give me your hand.'

'No that's me Lena, but that's okay.'

Frank laughed. 'Look, we gotta expect stuff like this, ya know. There were a good dozen black outs in the movie so we havta, ya know…expect em and accept em.'

'Christ, lucky there wasn't one when Katherine was driving.'

Inside was cold and the omnipresent hum was waiting for us. We shuffled in and heard the door squeak shut behind us.

The lights blinked on. There was even the occasional flicker across the 'screen' which momentarily morphed the 'scene' in and out of focus. It was a very professional job. There was a small desk just inside the doors. Sitting at the desk was Eileen from *Driveshaft*. She was inanimate, frozen in time it seemed. Her left hand was up in the air as if hailing a taxi. Eileen had nasty red puncture wounds either side of her neck. She wore a uniform, a blue and white chequered dress. And like Margot, she had two streams of blood which had flowed down in almost perfect symmetry onto her uniform.

Katherine walked up closer to Eileen. Above her head a fluorescent light flickered.

'What shall I do? Click my fingers?'

Lena squeezed my arm tight.

'Don't know, but I'm going to click my fucking heels in a minute. I wanna go home.'

Katherine clicked her fingers and as she did, a sound leaked into the atmosphere, like a projector whirring into life. Eileen also whirred into life, waved her left hand at us as she stood. Eileen was jolly—and like Eve—pretty vacant. She talked to us as if we weren't really there. Which I guess we weren't, really.

'Oh, Lord, well, look at you all…come on in outta that wet. it's so good that you've come. I told Jack you'd be here eventually. I told him that you all are good folk and that you wouldn't let us down. That's what I said. I said, Jack, they won't let us down. Sheriff Beale he told Jack the same. They'll come and put things right, he said. They're on a mission. Oh, look at you. That rain is never gonna stop until…you know…until it—this thing—is over. Anyway, I'll call Jack and he can take you along to your…the room. Jack! Jack, hun. They're here. Come on and show em the room, will ya?'

'Fuck…the room, not the room.'

Lena held me tighter.

Jack from *Driveshaft* waddled on to 'set'. He wore the same blue and white chequered uniform as his wife, in suit form. He also talked as if we were elsewhere.

Katherine nudged me. She sounded like an obsessive fan.

'It's surpassed itself. It must be because the four of us are together. What a performance. If I wasn't so bewildered, I would really be enjoying this.'

Frank agreed. 'Yeah, it's putting on a real show, all right, Kat.'

Jack walked up close to us. There was dried blood under his nose, around his mouth and chin.

'Howdy folks, yeah, I tried ta find Sheriff Beale, ya know…after we found…the body…his body in the office. We—that's me and Eileen—we took off. Beach, he didn't wanna come.'

Jack paused, eyed Frank curiously and then carried on.

'Anyway, I…oh, Eileen. I'm overcome. I caint tell it. Will ya carry on?'

Eileen's puncture wounds looked more gruesome as she walked around from her desk and into the light. She also looked much paler. The temperamental fluorescent light was a great touch as Eileen flickered in and out of darkness and light.

'Okay, Jack, hun. I'll tell em. Well, ya see, the plain truth is…is that we never found the Sheriff—on that side. We set out in the car, ya know, after we found what was left of him…the boss, ya know, down there, in that room. So, Beach, well he wouldn't come, ya know—'

Eileen paused, eyed Frank curiously and then carried on:

'Anyway, I think he, Beach, was talking to that strange girl. I can never quite recall her name…Jack just calls her the alien. She was for ever hiding herself in the toilet. Now ain't that strange? Anyway, we flew out past Beach, ya see, he didn't wanna come along. So…well the first surprise was that the goddam car actually worked. Oh, Jack, baby…I caint carry on.' Eileen sat back behind her desk. She put her small head in her small hands.

Jack picked up where she finished:

'Okay, Eileen, hun. So, we head out in the car, lookin' for Sheriff Beale. Well first thing we notice is this goddamn awful noise, like a hum, like in the air, ya know. Real creepy. Anyway, so we pass so many broke down cars…all over the place. I never knew there were so many cars in the damned territory…but…oh, I cain't go on, it cuts me deep. Eileen?'

Eileen continued to play verbal tag with Jack, the flickering bulb continued to flicker above her head.

'Okay, Jack, hun. Yeah, so…well, we ventually comes across Sheriff Beale's vehicle…ya know, abandoned like. So, we get out and start walking on over, when outta the blue comes this helicopter and, well…I swear ta ya it had no pilot. And it got so low and close to us we just had to run. Worse thing is that we runs different ways…and…and that's the last we seen of each other…ya know on…on that side. Then…well, I ran… and ran, I was so scairt an all. I just didn't stop running until…well, you see this car pulls up, red and white…Mustang I think it was with this…this…woman.'

'Wow…another revelation.'

'Yeah, those Mustangs are all over, it seems.'

Eileen started to break down: '—and…well…it …she—'

Jack went over and comforted Eileen.

'Love is all around. Even on the other side.'

'Guess so, Frank. Kind of comforting isn't it?'

'Eileen, they know. You don't have to tell em no more. It's why they're here. They know, Eileen.'

Eileen was balling into Jack's chest. Jack sat her down behind the desk and wandered back over to us. Eileen froze again with her left hand back in the air.

'Sorry 'bout that, folks. She's still very fragile. That car business…I mean…ouch. Look, my back ain't what it used ta be so just bring yer own stuff and follow me.'

We didn't have any stuff, but Jack led us down the corridor and we soon found ourselves in familiar territory. We were slowly headed towards the door with the frosted glass window and the grisly secret behind it. Jack was behind us, then he shrunk back into the darkness and was gone. I trailed slightly behind and paused at the toilet door that Margot had locked herself in. Lena walked back towards me.

An orange light leaked from under the toilet door and into the corridor. I stopped, held my breath and turned the handle. I was disappointed and relieved that it was locked.

'Great…just great. What would you have said to ole Margot, here in limbo-land, circa 1970 whatever? What would you have said to the poor fictional, doomed bitch?'

'I just wanted to…'

Lena mimicked me. 'I just wanted to…'

Frank almost laughed but his nervousness prevented it. He started to rub his legs.

'Hey, come on Lena, you got the green eyes now, girl.'

Finally, we were all gathered at the frosted glass door.

'Well, will we go in?'

'Hold it a sec.'

Lena held my arm tightly. She looked intensely serious.

'Somethings been brewing up here in this tiny attic.' Lena jabbed her forehead.

'Shoot, Lena darlin'.'

'Well, I know we have to go through with it; destiny, fate, finishing the job, etc…but why don't we imagine that it's an empty office or better still that it's a—I don't know—nice room with beds and satellite teevee.'

I't's a good idea, Lena. But it's just that Eve's daddy was in the film. I mean, we did see him at some point, and it is obvious that he is very dead behind this frosted glass door.'

'Yeah but we never saw it. Same as we never saw Sheriff Beale. Frank?'

'I dunno, darlin'. It's a tough one to call.'

Frank put his hand on the door handle.

Lena held me even tighter.

'Hold it. I've got it. Stick to the script. The door doesn't open in the film to show us the…remains so don't open the door. Let's just get the fuck out of here. We've helped Eve, we spoke to the…Sheriffs, we've met Jack and Eileen. We've made our fucking film. We've done the exorcism. Haven't we? That's it. I think this is dangerous territory. New territory, that we don't have to erm…I don't know what's the word.'

'Traverse.'

Katherine looked at Lena. Lena held on to Frank's hand—
the one on the handle of the frosted glass door.

'Maybe you're right. Perhaps we're overstepping the mark.'

'Yeah, save it for the sequel. That door could be the gateway
to the fucking abyss. Not that I believe in it, but…'

'But say if…it—the movie—isn't happy with that decision.
Thinks we welched on it, ya know. It might get ugly. And,
besides, Katherine's car is…broke.'

'Ah, but is it now?'

'Yeah, how about a bet, Frank?'

'Hold on.'

'What?'

'Listen.'

'To what?'

'Exactly, that hum has gone and—'

'No rain?'

'No rain.'

We turned in a collective act of—cowardice?—and headed
back towards the double-doors. I couldn't help but try the toilet
again. It was locked, again. Perhaps a good thing in the long run.

We walked past Eileen who, to me anyway, seemed to move
her hand in farewell. Opened and closed the squeaking double
doors.

The rain had stopped. The air was clear. We made our way
to Katherine's car. We got in. Frank said his legs felt better. Lena
went for her seatbelt, then changed her mind. Katherine told us
to cross our fingers. We did. The car started first time. We
would have driven past the *Driveshaft* building except it was no
longer there. In the car I elbowed Lena.

'You withheld.'

'What now?'

'You withheld. Didn't want to see the gore. Remember when we watched the film? You said that the director must have been a male because he decided not to show us the gore. You said he was on a power trip and was probably a premature ejaculator. Remember?'

'I haven't got the faintest idea what you are chatting about, fuck-face.'

Ritzy Cinema or Classic?

The sped-up, double-time thing kicked in again. Click, click, it clicked on by. Katherine's shit brown Volvo flashed through Kent and before we knew it, we were hitting the outskirts of London. There was hardly any traffic. The silence in the car was heavy, not uncomfortable— in fact the opposite. To me it felt like the weight of gravity had increased and became sweet. Nobody knew what to say which was weird and not weird. It felt sort of pointless recapping events. We all seemed to be mulling it all over, wondering whether what had happened had actually happened. How much of it was real, how much of it some collective fantasy. Lena held my hand all the way, making sure her seatbelt was secured firmly under her backside.

The dream in the car is one that will stay with me forever although I'd want the extended version if possible. There is Margot in full Amityville (thirty-two minutes in) mode; white blouse, white knickers/panties, shasta daisy behind her left ear; eyes big and bright and wide and alive with that little extra, and, of course, just one leg warmer. Margot is smiling her crooked and most suggestive smile, sauntering towards my dream self who is helplessly agog with lust:

```
Margot: Hey Benny, I wanna thank you so
much for all of the work you've put in.
Me: Oh, I—
Margot: Ssssshhh. Don't say another word.
Margot slowly slides her arms around my
neck. She looks up, smiling and cat-like
and starts to kiss my neck. Then Margot
```

…when I'm jolted awake by Lena snoring and dribbling on my neck.

'Shit.'

'Wassup, fuck-face.'

Lena yawned and wiped her mouth as I wiped her saliva from my neck.

'Oops. Sorry.'

Frank turned around and smiled. 'You know you were just talking in your sleep, Benny?'

'I wasn't, was I? I was?'

'You was.' Frank winked at me. 'Yeah, you were saying, oh, Lena, ah Lena…at last, at last.'

'Wow, what was I doing then, fuck-face?'

'Erm…I'll tell you later, Leen.'

I flushed. Lena gave me and Frank the stink-eye. I could see her ruminating and about to launch an attack when Katherine intervened. She looked slightly uncomfortable but, as ever, sounded in control.

'You want to see something neat?'

'Always, Kat. Go for it'.

'Okay, ready?'

Katherine took her hands from the steering wheel and held them in the air. Me and Lena lurched instinctively forward to grab the wheel. Frank laughed and stopped us.

'Frank, you nut, grab the wheel will you'.

'No need, Lena darling. This baby's taking us exactly where we need to go.'

'What the are you on about?'

Katherine's hands were still floating in space.

'Katherine, you're the sensible one. Grab that fucking steering wheel, please.'

'I can do Lena, but it makes no difference. The car's been in control ever since we left Dungeness.'

'That's right people and it's taking us towards the happy ending that we've planned so carefully.'

'Frank, no disrespect, but why the fuck are you being so…weird?'

'Cause it's all coming together nicely, Benny.'

Katherine cleared her throat and placed her hands back on the steering wheel.

'That's not all.'

'What? What's not all, Kat?'

'Well, there is oddness happening…*outside* the car too.'

Frank laughed again as me and Lena looked out of our respective back seat windows, but it was too dark and rainy. We wound down our windows in unison.

As I looked out left, Lena looked out right. I didn't notice anything unusual at first until we stopped at the traffic lights. There on a giant billboard was the giant Marlboro cigarette dude; lighting up, wearing his white Stetson. Then a butterscotch Granada (think Jack Regan, *Sweeney*) pulled up beside our shit-brown Volvo. The windows were wound down and *Don't go Breaking My Heart* blasted forth. The driver sang along. He turned towards the car but looked right through us.

On her side of the car, Lena was commentating, her head out the window in the wind and the rain: 'holy fuck, polo neck jumpers and flares; Jesus wept, afros and donkey jackets; bollocking arseholes, it's a fucking chopper.'

I slid over to Lena's window and saw a long-haired, long-bearded dude on a classic 70s red chopper bike. He, too, looked straight through us.

'Well, guess we're not really here.'

'So, this is … this is what … when?'

'I'd say about 1976, Lena.'

I had been transfixed by the round silver dustbins that sat outside the shabby houses when Lena jumped up and clapped her hands.

'Got it. I've fucking got it.'

'And that is the sound of the penny dropping.'

'Thanks, Frank.'

Frank was enjoying the whole spectacle. Katherine was now applying lipstick as the car pulled away when the lights changed.

'I don't need the lipstick, just wanted to, you know.'

I looked at Lena, bemused.

'What have you got? Please share because I'm a little lost.'

'Oh, poor baby.' Lena pinched my cheeks. 'We're heading back to the Ritzy to see the ending…*our* ending. We're going to see if the exorcism worked.'

'Holy fuck. What is that?'

The wind and the rain and the dark didn't help; made what we were all staring at look even worse than it was—and it was bad enough. But, we were also tired and kind of immune to shock after all that *Driveshaft* had put us through—days for me and Lena; years for Frank and Katherine. So, I guess we were prepared for anything.

We stepped warily out of the car outside the Town Hall, staring over the road at what we all thought would be The Ritzy. Except it wasn't. The Ritzy was boarded up and closed down. It looked sad, tired and defeated. My heart felt heavy as I looked at the torn posters on the wooden boards that covered the doors; the forgotten pallets and half-empty sandbags and a sidecar with an L-plate. Above the doors instead of the advertised films: broken florescent bulbs hanging down, lazy and depressed.

'What? Where's the fucking Ritzy? What…does it mean? Have we failed? Do we have to reshoot it? Is it because we didn't go through with it properly…didn't go into that room in Dungeness and see that dismembered corpse?'

'Woah, Benny, none of the above. This is how it should be. This is the Ritzy, or rather, this *was* the Ritzy and *is* The Classic. We're in 1976. This is one historically accurate dreamscape we're ghosting through. That sidecar was a cultural landmark.'

'Can we even get in?'

'Well, there's only one way to find out, Kat.'

We headed towards the road, but Lena hadn't moved.

'Hold on. Hold on. It's scoop time. This is going to put us on countless TV show couches; The One Show, Breakfast TV, Richard and Judy—are they still at it? Right stand right there, you fuckers.'

Lena pulled her mobile phone from her back pocket. Frowned and swore. Smacked the phone on her thigh. Frowned and swore some more.

'Fucker, no juice. Try yours.'

We did. None of us had any juice.

'This is also a very wise-arsed fucking dreamscape. Very precious about copyright.'

As we paused at the kerb an old Routemaster 159 swooshed through a huge roadside puddle and soaked our legs. The conductor held on to the white-pole blank-eyed.

We were about to cross the road when somebody cut the lights.

'Fuck, blackout, of course.'

'Now, that is an appropriate touch. The seventies was full of power cuts.'

'So, was that fucking film. Should have been called blackout. How long will we have to—'

The lights snapped back on quickly. The lifeless fluorescent bulbs above the doors had been replaced by blinking red neon capitals:

DRIVESHAFT: **FOR ONE NIGHT ONLY**

'Now that's an invitation.'

Driveshaft Redux: A New Ending

We linked hands and crossed the road. Two enormous men with enormous afros sort of glided by us. Lena waved frantically but we were dead to them. We walked through the doors of The Classic. The foyer was cold, dark and empty. Rain from the leaky roof splashed and echoed all around us. A dim orange glow hovered around the black double doors that led to the main—and only—screen. Frank led the way into the empty auditorium. The ceiling lights were on low beam and barely illuminated the tattered red velvet seats. The orange glow now pulsed gently around the huge screen in front of us. Frank led us to the row, four from the front. Always my favourite spot.

As we sat, the projector whirred into life behind us. The film had begun. Our happy ending. Dungeness *Driveshaft*. We had come to see whether the exorcism had worked.

```
Blackout.

During the blackout we hear the sound of
a car engine slowly getting louder. Fade
to close-up of Margot in driver's seat.
Cut to her shaking hand turning on the
radio. We hear Beacham's voice as we cut
to Margot who listens intently.

Hey, Margot, Beacham from beyond…again.
Shit, it's not like I haven't got stuff
to do. Anyway, glad that ya tuned in
again, girl. There is a way to bring this
curse to an end…but you gotta be super-
```

quick, girl…ya hear me? Stop nodding, I caint see ya. When you pick up the hitcher, and there will be one, you both gotta work together, ya know. You gotta convince…this woman that she needs to work with ya, okay? So, like previous, ya send her to the trunk to collect, well you know what's in there but, remember, she doesn't…so, be kindly. Anyhow, move over and when she comes back with the…object, get her to place it in the driver's seat…and when that seat belt straps that thing in, you skedaddle out the passenger door to freedom and this here vehicle screeches off into the sunset. The end. Good luck, Margot. Hope I don't see ya for a long while.

Cut to interior windscreen shot as Margot sees sign for Ringo's Diner. She gasps as she sees Eve running towards the car. Cut to bird's-eye shot. It looks as though the car will hit Eve until it screeches into a 360-degree turn and stops. The engine throbs menacingly. Cut to Margot as she watches Eve run towards the car. Cut to mid-shot. We see front view of car. Eve runs to the passenger door.

Margot (screams): Eve, stop right there, baby. Don't…don't you touch this car till I tell you when. Y'understand me, baby?

Eve (Baffled, wide-eyed. Pulls up urgently at Margot's distress): Okay. Sure…sure, I understand.
Margot: Listen, now, Eve…and do as I say…exactly. Okay, baby?
Eve: Okay, but I thought we were going to LA.

Eve backs away from the car, spots the blood on Margot's dress and her general dishevelment.

Eve (Distressed, beginning to weep): Margot, what the hell happened? All that blood.

Cut to Margot.

Margot: Sokay…I'm okay, baby…but you have to do just as I say… then…then we'll head to LA. Y'understand me, Eve?

Cut to Eve.

Eve: Okay, baby.

Cut to close-up of Margot.

Margot: Okay, Eve, this is all kinds of freaky and it's gonna hurt ya, but…listen carefully, I want you to go to the trunk, okay?

Cut to Eve, looking puzzled.

Eve: Okay.

Cut to close up of Margot.

Margot: Good, baby…now when you get there, you'll find something that ain't nice, so I want you to prepare yourself. Eve, it ain't nice…what's in the trunk, okay?
Eve: Okay…okay. I get it.

Cut to Margot.

Margot: The thing…in the trunk, it's heavy, Eve, so you gotta be strong, baby. I know you are, but you're gonna have to use all your strength to bring it…this thing from the trunk…okay, Eve?

Cut to Eve.

Eve: Okay…why can't you help me, baby?

Cut to Margot.

Margot: I can't…I just can't leave this car yet. I just can't, that's all. You gotta trust me. You trust me Eve, doncha?

Cut to Eve

Eve: I trust you, baby.

Cut to shot of car in middle of frame. Camera is still as we view what follows. We see Margot biting her lip, crying. We can just see Eve go to the back of the car through both windscreens—as Margot did earlier. Eve disappears from view as the trunk opens. She screams very loudly as Margot's expression is one of anguish and then immense relief, as the seat-belt snaps loose. Margot moves over into the passenger seat.
Eve is in hysterics as Margot talks to her above the throbbing engine noise. Close up on Margot.

Margot: Eve, listen, drag him…drag it outta there, baby…and bring it up here. It's heavy, baby…but you…we gotta do this.
Eve (weeping, childlike voice): What the…why did you…why did you bring him here?
Margot: It…it doesn't matter, baby. I just hadta. Just do as I say.
Eve (Groaning, straining, crying): I…I can't lift him…he's…it's…too heavy, baby.
Margot: Eve, if you don't do this we'll never get outta here. We'll never get to LA. It's that simple. Ya hear me, Eve?

We feel everything through Margot's very obvious distress. We hear a heavy thud from the back of the car. Eve closes the trunk and we can just about see her tear-stained face over Margot's shoulder, through the windscreens. Slight zoom out so that we see Eve come into view at the side of the car. Her back is to us. We cannot see what she is dragging. Eve is crying, straining, groaning. We hear the sound of something scraping along the ground.

Margot: Good, baby…that's good, Eve. Now, open the door, the driver's door, Eve and drag…him…it…into the seat. I can help a little…but I can't leave this car, yet.

As Eve opens the driver's door, we hear the whir of approaching chopper blades. Cut to helicopter looking down at the car. We see Eve struggling with the unidentified heavy object which we're pretty sure is Margot's ex-boss/Eve's father—but, tantalizingly, we can't quite see. Eve manages to get it into the driver's seat, assisted by Margot. Cut to medium shot of Margot in passenger seat.

Margot: That's it, Eve. You've done it. Now, shut the door, when I count to three, okay, baby?
Eve: Okay.
Margot: One…two…three.

As the door shuts, we cut to back of car. Margot dives from the car as it screeches

away with the passenger door open. Eve runs to Margot. They embrace. Cut to Margot and Eve as they watch the car speeding away, out of control. It veers off the road and out of shot. We hear an explosion. Then we see a ball of flame, followed by black smoke. Cut to medium shot of pilotless helicopter at our eye-level. Cut to helicopter watching burning wreckage up the road from the embracing couple.
Zoom in on the lovers. The camera swirls around them. Pauses on Margot's face. She stares straight into the camera. Freeze.

Blackout.

Back to the Future Now

The first indication that we were back in the real world was a disgruntled voice that echoed around us.

'I don't know, man, they must be drunk or stoned or something. I'm not going near them. I've had enough of weirdos for one day. It's your turn.'

'How many of them?'

'Four, and they're all out of it…on something, defo.'

'Shit. Can't we both go?'

'All right. Suppose you wanna hold my hand, do you?'

'Fuck you. Come on. Let's go.'

We were rudely jolted out of whatever blackout we were in when the two Ritzy staff members shook us back to, what we hoped, was reality and politely told us to vacate the premises. We apologised and struggled to our feet. I led the way this time, with Frank at the rear.

'Guess what? I've only got pins and needles.'

Lena's response was, as usual, direct but spot on. 'Yeah but, Frankie, that's because you've been on your arse for fuck knows how long.'

'Probably right there, girl. Christ, I could murder a whisky.'

It was clear almost immediately that we were in new, trendy, corporate Ritzy 2019 and not The Classic in 1976. As we left screen one, I looked up at the cornice, nudged Lena.

'Oh, what do you call it…that word…to do with starting something off…oh, fuck…'

'Catalyst?'

We both smiled. Held hands and kissed.

The light was white and blinding as the two guys held the black doors open for us. They didn't squeak. We made our way up to the upstairs bar. Our legs were heavy. It was hard to summon the energy to talk. It had stopped raining.

In the upstairs bar, we sat outside in a rough circle of barstools around a table. We looked over at new Brixton; safer and shinier, but duller. We were dazed and inert but there was a palpable sense of triumph, or maybe relief fits better, hovering around us. Frank had already finished his whisky and was about to get up to get some more. He paused as he got to his feet. Gave his thighs a good slap.

'Ah, they've gone. The legs feel good. Same again?'

Lena finished her drink and put it back on the table.

'I thought that was a fucking superb ending. Easily the best part of the film.'

'Academy award standard.'

Lena pointed out a young couple who could easily have been from the mid-70s; big collars, chunky corduroy slacks, but it was a soulless imitation. Frank returned with even larger whiskies. He slid them over to us and sat.

'You know what's going to happen now, don't you?'

'What?'

'We're gonna be annoyed that it's gone. If it has, that is. You know, like when a car alarm has been going for ages then stops. You sort of miss it, you know?'

Lena shook her head.

'No, Frank. I might miss it later on down the road, but now… I'm just glad it's all over. I just want to get pissed.'

'Cheers to that.'

Gradually a whirring noise invaded our peace. A helicopter slowly hove into view above the town hall clock. We all lurched forward, then looked at one another. Lena pulled her sunglasses from her bag, put them on and looked up at the chopper.

'Fuck me, I hope there's a pilot in that thing?'

Epilogue

Things never really returned to normal. Like I said, at the top, I didn't go back to school to get myself squashed again. After welching on the deal, I was greeted with shaking heads, raised eyebrows, ringing hands: What about the kids? Those kids need you. You can't leave them, etc, etc. Fuck the kids, said Lena. Forget them. They've forgotten you. Forget them. So, I did.

Lena and me are still plodding along. She has moved a bit closer; three doors away. We talked—or more accurately I talked—about having kids. Lena said that our combined genes would probably produce the missing link who'd be a bo-ho drifter, a film director or a serial killer. So, instead, we got a cat and called it Margot.

We have occasional reunions with Katherine and Frank. We catch a film, reminisce and get drunk on whisky. Neither of us ever had any *Driveshaft* moments again.

I'd like to finish on an archetypal 70s horror film note—just when you thought it was over, etc—but there was no more otherworldliness. Apart from life with Lena. Oh, and this weird moment when our postman, Brian, knocked on the door one Saturday morning.

'Ello mate, how ya doin'?'

'Yeah, good. Bit early, Brian.'

'Yeah, sorry about that.'

Brian started to fumble around in his blue and red satchel.

'Old on a sec, mate. Ah, 'ere we go. Just wanted to run this by ya.'

Brian held up a postcard, turned it over in his hands.

'This has been doin' the rounds—'scuse the phrase—in South London sorting offices for months. Anyway, it arrived on my frame the other day and I thought of you and yer missus.'

Brian handed me the postcard.

'Yeah, there's nothing in the address panel but…look at what it says there.'

Brian held his index finger under *Lena and her sweet friends.*

'That's what put me in mind of you and your bird…erm, sorry…missus. It is Lena, innit?'

I frowned and turned it over and received a jolt in my gut. The postcard was a collage of L.A landmarks. My eye hovered over the child-like writing and the name at the bottom, *Eve.*

'Fuck.'

'Yeah, thought so. Yours innit?'

'I…yeah, well, I think so. Thanks, Brian.'

Brian hung around, smiling, waiting for a little something.

'Tell you what, Brian, drop by on Monday morning and I'll have some of those IPAs you love.'

'Oh no need mate…what time?'

'Tennish?'

'See ya then.'

Lena was sitting on the stairs, stroking Margot.

'What's that?'

'It's a wind up, must be.'

I sat next to Lena, showed her the postcard.

'Who's it from?'

I showed her the card.

'Ha-ha. It's Frank, got to be.'

'Yeah, that was my first thought.'

'Read it out then, fuck-face.'

I cleared my throat and did a scratchy North American accent:

To Lena and her sweet friends,
Just wanted to say thanks again for saving me on the road and dropping me in LA. We're doing ok in LA just like Margot said we would.
I'm working in a sweet little diner. The tips are great and everyone is real nice—even the boss! Margot is making it as an actress. She's got this big role coming up soon. Think she's gonna make it. Just gotta good feeling about it.
Anyway, gotta get back to the griddle.
Thanks again. Lord bless ya.
Love Eve and Margot.
Xx

Lena laughed.
'That's got Frank written all over it.'
'Definitely, Frank.'
'Yeah.'

WriteSideLeft

2019

www.writesideleft.com